In the End

Short Fiction
by
Lori L. Schafer

CONTENTS

CONTENTS

iv

ACKNOWLEDGMENTS

"Among the Snowdrops" originally appeared in *The Journal of Microliterature* on November 30, 2014.

"Ocean View" originally appeared in *The Journal of Microliterature* on February 1, 2015.

"The Watchers" originally appeared in the September 2014 issue of *Avalon Literary Review.*

"Fluffy Robes and Slippers" originally appeared in *Every Day Fiction* on November 28, 2013.

"The Autocrat" originally appeared in *Flash Fiction Magazine* on June 9, 2014.

"Squirrel Revolution" originally appeared in *Separate Worlds* in July 2013.

"Beach House" originally appeared in *Romance Flash* on January 15, 2015.

"Night Falls" originally appeared in *Every Writer's Resource* on January 19, 2014.

"Poisoned" originally appeared in *The Journal of Microliterature* on November 4, 2013.

"State of Micronesia, 2016" originally appeared in *Every Day Fiction* on September 23, 2014.

AMONG THE SNOWDROPS

Gretchen shuddered as the train edged noisily away; tried and failed to forget where it had come from, where it was going. Hard-hitting snowflakes assailed her hair and cap, dotting her form with bits of frost that refused to melt, that clung tightly to her as if content to wait for spring to come.

She trudged painfully through the deep snow covering the sidewalk, shivering in spite of the long woolen coat, the thick-knit gloves, the fleece-lined boots in which her feet were comfortably entrenched. She could not have imagined how terrible, how terrifying this winter would be.

The caretaker was waiting at the house when she arrived, rubbing the gnarled hands she recalled from her youth over a warm, cheerful fire. Hands now aged, blotched with spots; hands that had faithfully spent the last forty years in her mother's service.

"She kept up the garden real nice," he assured her kindly. "Right until the end."

Well she remembered her mother's garden. The loving care with which she'd tended it, tilling the soil before the frost had truly gone, coaxing flowers up out of the dirt before the sun had barely begun to shine through the winter clouds.

"Did she suffer?" she asked abruptly. "At the end?"

"No," he answered slowly. "No, I don't believe she suffered much."

Gretchen bowed her head and gazed out the wide, wintry window, at a world cloaked in white, punctuated only by the bare brown branches of naked trees poking up through the snow, ice crystallizing each limb from tip to stem.

"No one blames you," the caretaker said softly. "For leaving her. All other things aside, she was…" He swallowed in the sudden silence. "A very cold woman."

Yes, a cold woman, she thought, bidding him farewell in the bitter chill that froze her breath and numbed her fingers, the cold to which she thought she could never again become accustomed. The cold she had left behind.

She couldn't help but remember, as she sat now by the hot, glowing fire, how her mother had so earnestly described it, that one night four decades before, when Gretchen herself had been scarcely more than a child. How she'd breathed deeply and relayed the entire story at once, as if she'd been holding it carefully in reserve, waiting for her daughter to be old enough to listen to it. The trains arriving one after another, crammed to their icicle-laden rafters. The passengers disembarking, standing shivering in the winter snow. The orders being given to undress, to run naked on frostbitten feet before the selection staff. The frozen barracks, their bunks jammed tight, ever tighter with women, ever more sick prisoners, more starving inmates. The cracks of the whip and the sadism of the guards wielding it; the insistence of the block-leaders on wielding it while its victim stood bare-backed in the chill wind that blew here, through Oswiecim, through Auschwitz.

The block-leaders, she thought, her stomach sickening at the recollection as she stared about her mother's warm, welcoming house with its quaint, outmoded furniture, its thick, heavy drapes, its bright, cheerful windows opening onto the garden, where in spring she had liked to watch the flowers growing up out of the frost.

She heard a thump from somewhere outside, as of a bottle of milk, a newspaper being delivered to their doorstep, a peaceful sound out of her childhood days, before she'd heard her mother's story. Before a thump brought to mind the evil images, of men in uniforms come to drag the innocents away, men and women and young girls, just like her, just like she had been.

She tiptoed to the front door; opened it guardedly against the wind and snow that swirled even harder in the descending nightfall, against the cold that penetrated her defenseless skin. In the darkling dusk she discerned two trails of ragged footprints penetrating the snow, leading to and from the porch in hapless, unsteady array, as if made by a man uncertain of his errand, unsure of his way. The source of the sound lay at her feet, a small pot containing a cluster of tiny white flowers. Galanthus nivalis, she thought, automatically recalling the scientific nomenclature for the flower that bloomed first in the spring, that survived even the late snows. How proud her mother had been to refer to it that way; how she'd scorned the native term.

She bent to retrieve it and descried a note tied to the slender stalk, a scrap of snow-dampened paper fluttering in the icy air, a coarse handful of block-letters etched upon it in quivering ink. She retreated inside and closed the door behind her, shutting out the terrible, terrifying cold.

"For the funeral," she read.

Perhaps some had learned to look past it, to see her mother only as the mild old lady gently tending her garden, caressing the fragile petals and stems of her beloved plants with delicate fingers, as if fearful of doing them harm.

Perhaps some could forget, could feel sorrow over an elderly woman's passing, compassion for the long-lost daughter who would suffer and mourn at her death. Or perhaps there were no longer any remaining, of those who had known her before.

She turned to gaze at it, her mother's most prized possession, the treasured photograph, still standing proudly on the polished end-table by the sofa where she had liked to sit. Her mother, young and pretty in her SS uniform, smiling brightly at the camera as if untroubled by either cares or conscience. And meticulously arranged in a vase beside her, her mother's favorite: snowdrops, the flower that disdains the cold, and survives the frost.

Tomorrow, after the funeral, she would return. Take the flowers and leave them there, in remembrance of the thousands, the tens and hundreds of thousands who had stood waiting with their feet buried in snow to learn whether they would live or die. Those who had waited in vain among the snowdrops for the spring to come.

Imagine waking up one day and discovering that your mother or father was a serial killer, a torturer in the employ of a brutal dictatorship, or a violent criminal whose "work" has led to the death of innocent children. There must be many such sons and daughters confronting those horrifying realizations, and, for the German generation that was born in the final years and aftermath of the Third Reich, it must have been a common story indeed.

In addition to the Nazi leaders whose names are well known, thousands of ordinary men and women were employed in the massive bureaucracy that engineered and managed the Holocaust, and much study has been made of their motivations, of the means by which they morally justified their actions, and even of their eventual reabsorption into post-war German society. Yet comparatively little has been said regarding their children, each of whom, must, at some point, have discovered that the man or woman they loved and respected had been a participant in arguably the greatest tragedy in history. How does a child reconcile the image of a parent they know as gentle and doting with the picture of one screaming "Schnell! Schneller!" at starving concentration camp inmates while wielding a whip? How many young people have listened to their elderly grandparents regale them with tales of the "good old days" only to later discover that they meant the Nazi regime?

Although the image of Magda Goebbels poisoning her six children in the bunker beneath Berlin as the Russians invaded fills us with pity and horror for the innocent victims, one can't help but wonder what kind of lives they would have led, growing up in the shadow of the crimes of their father. What life would have awaited Hitler's sons and daughters, if he had had them? Would they have defended or even glorified their father, like Gudrun Burwitz, daughter of Heinrich Himmler, who, seventy years later, is still a staunch supporter of Nazi ideology and a hero of the neo-Nazi movement? Few, I think, could maintain such a stance. Most, I suspect, would prefer to simply forget the troubling history of the older generation, because the participants in the massacre we know as the Holocaust were once so ubiquitous and so widespread that their children could not have rejected them, as Gretchen in this story rejected her mother. The former low-level Nazis were rarely shunned or ostracized by their society; by and large they returned to their lives, as did their parents and brothers and sisters and yes, even their children.

Somewhere in Germany a very old woman sits and

examines a photograph of herself or her young husband in uniform and remembers those days as the best time of her life. In so many ways, she is no different from any other elderly lady who fondly recalls her era of youth, and this is what we must find so disturbing. Because she does not look like a criminal, and she does not seem sadistic or evil; she is merely an old woman who works in her garden and has tea with her neighbors, and her "colorful" past has been graciously forgotten. But sometimes let us stop, let us look at her and remember how easy it can be to forget, how much more comfortable it can be to disregard what we don't wish to remember. And let us take flowers from her carefully tended garden and place them on the graves where they truly belong.

OCEAN VIEW

She rocks, the antiquated chair creaking quietly against the worn wood of the porch. The sun blazes high overhead and she pauses; bends to steal a sip of lemonade, pink from the pitcher on the table beside her.

"So what do you think, Ma?" He nudges her back into consciousness, awareness of his presence.

She reflects, scrutinizing her son, seated still at her feet, nearly aged himself now: back bent, head bald, beard white. Just like his father, God rest his soul.

"I always wanted to live by the ocean," she replies, turning away from him to face it again: the calm azure horizon, the warm gentle breakers foaming white off the shore.

"I know you did," he says, turning, too. Seabirds scuttle back and forth across the muddy beach, forcing their beaks into the saturated earth when the waves retreat; retreating themselves when the wet wash returns.

She continues to rock, clasps her hands tight in her lap as she watches, thinking sadly of Herbert, the view they might have shared had he only lived longer.

"It's lovely," she admits at last. "But I don't like having so many new people in town."

Herbert Jr. leans back on his callused palms; extends his lanky legs down over the wide wooden steps, the familiar front stoop of his long-ago youth.

"They had to go somewhere," he reminds her gently.

"I suppose," she concedes. "But I do hope they'll go home soon."

He peers worriedly into the gray fog of his mother's eyes. "They can't go home, Ma. Remember I told you? Their houses are underwater now."

"Still?" she inquires, astonished. "But it's been so long."

He swallows. "Don't you remember, Ma? I told you what happened, with the sea level and all…"

"Laziness, pure laziness!" she sputters, an old fire rekindling itself in her cool clouded eyes. "In my day we knew how to work, how to rebuild after a catastrophe. Why, when your father came back from the war…"

He allows her to ramble while he again seeks the sea; descries the encampment at the foot of the dunes to the north, the shanty-town set upon the cliff to the south. For once he is grateful that her sight has grown dim.

"…There wasn't a country in the world that could match us for productivity! We were proud to be Americans, proud to belong to these fifty states!"

"Forty-seven," Herbert sighs without thinking.

She ceases rocking, cold choler in her countenance. "I'm not senile, Herbert. You think I don't know how many states there are?"

"Sorry, Ma," he answers contritely.

She sips her lemonade sourly. "You should be," she agrees. "I suppose next you'll be telling me it isn't awfully warm for November?"

"No, Ma. You're absolutely right; it is awfully warm for November."

She resumes her rocking, a bit more fiercely; squints past her son at the calm azure coast, the light tranquil breakers, the warm gentle waves lapping ever nearer, ever closer to the old family home.

The phenomenon of climate change has given rise to a relatively new genre of fiction known as "cli-fi," in which writers explore the possible outcomes of a variety of scenarios involving global weather patterns. Whether you believe that climate change is man-made or a part of the natural cycle of our planet's warming and cooling, I think we can all agree that our climate is changing, and that, as occurred during the Ice Age, these changes may have substantial if not devastating effects on our civilization. Because weather is not merely weather, of course, a scale that measures our physical comfort; it also determines what food we can grow, and where we can live, and how prone we are to go to war with other nations when the resources we crave are no longer available.

I personally always envision a story in which astronauts investigate our neighboring Venus, with its thick layer of greenhouse gases and blazing hot, uninhabitable surface. What if it turned out that there had once been life there; an ancient civilization that destroyed itself with fossil fuels and exhaust long before ours did? I can almost picture Charlton Heston, in a moment straight out of *Planet of the Apes*, realizing that what happened there is happening here, dropping to his knees and crying "You maniacs! You blew it up! Ah, damn you! God damn you all to hell!"

But of course the reality will be far less dramatic and far less fascinating than the stories we can imagine. Here in the U.S., the reality will be a gradual loss of coastal land and the slow displacement of persons into the sparsely populated interior of our country. It will require changes in allocations of natural resources and labor as different forms of agriculture rise in importance and new types of technology become vital to our continued existence. It will mean shifts in our populations, away from the now bitter cold invading the central parts of our nation and Canada, and away from the West Coast, where the ongoing drought in California will make life unsustainable for the currently vast number of residents unless drastic measures are taken. It will almost certainly negatively affect our standards of living, as prices will rise even while demands are increasing. But, barring a Venus-like planetary disaster, it is likely that we will survive, that we as a species will find ways to survive.

But I think it will be very difficult and very unpleasant, and I, for one, envy that short-sighted elderly woman who sits on her porch, unaware of what's transpiring around her, living in the comparative peace of not knowing. Clinging, as we have too long, to the presumption that life as we knew it would always continue, that change couldn't come unless we desired it.

BROKEN

The watch had stopped. It ticked no more; its one remaining hand had ceased to turn; the glass of its face was cracked and broken.

She couldn't stop staring at it, the now-useless timepiece with its motionless arm and shattered visage. Where was the other hand? she wondered, kneeling on the concrete beside it. Only the minute remained; the hour was gone. She searched about, sought it; finally perceived it glinting in a crack of the sidewalk, the precious piece nearly lost. Pried it out and held it, an inert sliver of time, a hand in her hand. As if hoping one day to reattach it, to fix what was broken, get it working again.

The band, too, was scratched and deformed, its silvery plates marred and misaligned. She reached out and tried gently to smooth them, to burnish the metal with tender fingers, to snap the links back into order. They resisted, twisted further out of position, defying her effort, resenting her intrusion.

She surrendered. Removed her eyes from the clock on the sidewalk and sought time overhead in the heavens instead. Glanced up at it, at the bright glowing sun that bathed the street with its warmth and its light, that reflected its rays off the splinters in the face of the watch and the bends in the joints of its band. Gazed blankly at the crowd, which milled about muttering, staring too at the watch where it lay fractured and crushed. Perceived the profiles of policemen, grimly lining the barren street and busy sidewalk, protecting the scene, guarding its perimeter. Seeking the criminal responsible, the source of the breakage. Lost sight of them in the shadow, the clandestine covered entrance of a tall modern building, the complex containing the office where her husband had worked.

She turned back to the concrete, the hard, unfriendly surface that had refused to bow, declined to give. Whose power had conquered, overcome mere platinum and glass. Which still held its victim, displayed it in warning, in stone-faced defiance of her wish and her will.

It was still broken, still motionless and silent, the watch and the body to which it was so firmly attached. The joints twisted and mangled, scarred and bent back. The faces shattered and splintered, beyond restoration, beyond hope of repair. The ticking was done. Only the minute remained now; the hour was gone.

DARKNESS COMES

It was growing dark.

The scientists had warned them it would; their ancient ancestors had known, countless millions of years before, about the coming darkness. But in the vague vastness of astronomical time it had always seemed distant, unimportant; who knew if the species would even still exist when it finally came? Whether any thinking being would be alive to witness it? But if it did, and there was, then someone would one day know, would see it; there would have to be a generation that lived it.

He often wondered what it would be like, at the very end. A few of those who had gone had left traces; sparse, meager tales foreshadowing their doom. His own great-great-great-grandfather had been alive when their astronauts had intercepted a missive from a planet called Earth, discovered aboard an antiquated spaceship that floated more than flew in the vacuum of space.

"Our sun is expanding. Soon it will swallow us up. We have nowhere else to go. Earth was here." A simple, almost childish message, easily decoded, readily understood. A three-dimensional projection map, pinpointing their position in the galaxy. And a computerized recording, replaying images of the Earthlings working, playing, living, loving. All that was left of the planet and its inhabitants.

Earth was here.

He had carried on the noble tradition of tracing them, the stars that were winking out all over the galaxy. He knew, of course, that by the time their dying light reached his powerful telescope that they were already long gone, sometimes millions of years gone, but still it saddened him, as if the loss were fresh and new, and not merely a memory consigned to a cold and distant past. As if another dear friend had only yesterday bidden him forever farewell and gone underground.

Sometimes when he was feeling melancholy he would pull up the old scans, the images from the generations before. Would compare them to the present ones, noting how much dimmer the night had become since they had begun tracking it. And find himself unable to count the number of dark chasms that had replaced the pinpricks of light that had once littered the night sky like so many sparkling jewels. Unwilling to know how many thousands had to vanish before only these few hundred remained.

Late one evening he had abandoned his dark and lonely post on the planet's surface, descended from the warm, well-insulated observatory to the cool, well-lit subterranean archives, retrieved the replica of the message from Earth, the most recent to have found them, and located the former planet's position in their own digital records. Had focused in on it, on its assigned space in the heavens, had sequenced rapidly through thousands of scans, scans twinkling with brightness and starlight seemingly without end. A prolonged series of nearly identical images at last giving way to a brief ball of red fire. And then to nothingness. Nothing that even their most advanced instruments could detect, even of a system in their own galaxy.

It had been a planet much like their own, circling a sun

of the same class, the same size, the same inevitable conclusion. They would suffer a similar fate; would watch as the boundary between planet and star grew thinner and warmer and ultimately vanished. They too would know.

The scientists couldn't predict with exactitude when it would happen to them. When the growing heat which had already driven their people underground would sear their planet beyond habitability. In what year their sun would be far enough along the path of its own evolution to envelop them entirely. But their calculations told them that it would be soon, very soon. Perhaps even in his own lifetime, were he to live it. He might, in his old age, be its lonely witness, a solitary man on the solitary surface of a solitary planet, seeing the light and feeling the heat signaling the end.

It had happened on other worlds, many of them, he knew. But the sky was so dark now that he suspected that theirs was one of the last to go. It was not only their world that was ending. The universe was ending, too. It was coming at last. The end of all things. All but the darkness.

They had a message ready, too, in case anyone anywhere lingered long enough to receive it. Digitized images of their own people at work and at play and at life and at love. A map of their position in the galaxy. A few meaningless words describing their fate, a fate that those who read them must one day inevitably share. Soon it would be time to release the capsule containing it. We were here, it would cry out into empty space, into the growing darkness. We were here.

BROTHER NO MORE

We buried Mary on a Sunday. How pretty she looked, in her pleated white dress and her polished church shoes. Mama had wound pink ribbons all throughout her charcoal-black hair. My sweet kid sister, all wrapped up in pink and white, like a gift to the angels. You couldn't see the hole in the back of her head. But we all knew it was there.

All night I had lain awake, listening to Mama baking pies for the reception. The soft plop of the dough on the counter, the hard chop of the knife on the board. The squeak of the rack as she pulled a pan from the oven. The squeal of a sob as it tugged at her throat. She'd been crying ever since we'd left Mary downtown at the morgue. I wondered if she would ever stop crying.

Near dawn it grew quiet. I found Mama standing at the sink, poised motionless over a heap of powder-coated dishes.

"I'll wash them, Mama," I offered. Her spine stiffened, but she didn't turn around. She hadn't looked at me once since Mary died.

"Mama?"

"Get out, George," she croaked.

My jacket was hanging on the back of the chair where I had left it. The shoulders were dusty with floury fingerprints. I didn't brush them off.

"I'll be back for the funeral," I mumbled. Mama didn't answer.

It was a long walk to the silent square of concrete on which Mary had spent the last minute of her life. I stood on it, waiting.

"Take me downtown, George," she'd pleaded. "Mama won't let me go alone."

I hadn't wanted to take her. It wasn't my turf, and I knew it was trouble. But I never could resist playing big brother to Mary. Her eyes, always so soft and sad and helpless. Her still-girlish face, framed with pink ribbons, like a gift from the angels. And a hole in the back of her head that should have been mine.

I remembered how it had crept up beside us, thick and black as night, crude and slick as an oil spill. Maybe if I waited long enough, it would come to bury me, too.

Mama was sitting at the kitchen table when I returned, her face in her hands. I glanced at the stacks of envelopes surrounding her. I dug into my pocket and drew out a handful of hundred-dollar bills, fresh and crisp, like Mary's last dress.

"Don't worry, Mama," I murmured. "I can pay for the funeral."

Very slowly, she pushed her chair away from the table and rose to face me. For the first time since Mary died, she looked at me. Her eyes were soft, sad, helpless. Red, like Mary's blood on the sidewalk. And dark, like the windows of the sedan from which Mary had been shot.

For the first time in days, she reached for me. Extended a raw-knuckled hand and slapped me hard across the face. I let her.

I let her.

***

"Brother No More" is a flash fiction version of a long short story I originally wrote for the Story Share Literacy Project. The project seeks to make beginning and intermediate level books available to teens who struggle with reading, but with a twist – they specifically seek stories centered on themes that would appeal to a young adult audience. It's a brilliant concept. Imagine being a teenager who is trying to improve his or her reading, but the only books you can successfully work through on your own are directed at children. It's easy to see how bored and frustrated you would get with Dr. Seuss and The Berenstain Bears, which would certainly impede those readers' progress towards more meaningful literacy.

Such a book, however, in my experience, is not easy to write. Young adults at low reading skills levels are in a very different position from young children at the same level. They grasp much more complicated concepts and are interested in exploring more intricate themes, but for the writer, conveying such ideas in simplistic language and short, manageable sentences can be challenging indeed. On the other hand, because a typical teenager has a far more sophisticated oral vocabulary than a young child, it also behooves the writer to make limited use of words that might prove too difficult for younger readers.

Arduous as it was, I did find the process very rewarding, and I really enjoyed the story itself, which details George's journey towards acceptance of what happened to Mary and how her death prompts him to seek a new life. This flash fiction piece closely resembles the first chapter of the Story Share "Brother No More," except that I took larger liberties with style and language and went to great pains to reconstruct it as a short and self-contained story. However, it is interesting to note that, as flash fiction, the style is of writing is still actually quite similar to that of the longer piece, with short, crisp, sentences and limited use of modifying adjectives and adverbs. When I one day write the next segment of George and Mary's story, I will definitely consider flash fiction as a useful guide for composing short work for older beginning readers.

THE WATCHERS

He lingers by the cyclone fence, his mottled hands clasping the diagonal squares of wires twisted and coiled about each other in stern defense of the treasures inside, his chest pressing against the sharp edges of the steel barbs adorning its apex, high enough to prevent a child from escaping, low enough to permit an agile young man to vault it in an instant.

He watches. All is stillness and silence; a cool, late autumn sun hovers in the pallid sky behind him, casting his long somber shadow into the playground, into the yard. The shadow permitted entrance, the man not.

He releases his grip, sighs and shifts position; kneels down into a crouch, collapsing his shadow, cloaking it; compressing it from an elongated dimness into a dull ball of dark on the sidewalk beneath.

And then he sees him, the other onlooker, the other young man hanging by the fence on nearly the opposite side of the schoolyard, so bold, so confident; not even deigning to duck as the bell sounds its warning, its foreshadowing of the flood shortly to pour forth from its doors.

John moves quickly, sacrificing stealth for speed, having only seconds, half a minute in which to act. He checks his legs, forces them not to run; to walk briskly instead, like a man who is late but not yet alarmed. He strides breathlessly, purposefully around the perimeter, his left hand free and swinging, his right cupping the cold steel in his pocket.

But he is too late; the dam has burst and the other man has tensed, stood taller, leaned harder against the fence, and a child has diverted from the bubbling stream, a little girl in pink and purple, and she is rushing away from the teachers, the students, the crowd, almost as if drawn, pulled irresistibly into peril, threatening to overflow the banks of the river of children and muddy herself irrevocably on the shore.

He surrenders. Discards feigned disinterest and breaks into a gallop, releasing his weapon, relying on the force of his body alone. But the other man doesn't notice, he is too focused; calling to the child, summoning her to the fence, smiling as she clutches it with miniature fingers. Abruptly he frowns, failing to comprehend when the girl glances, astonished and scared, towards the impervious missile hurtling towards them.

"Daddy, look out!" she cries, and the other man whips his head around, watches John falter to a stumbling halt in the center of the sidewalk, panting and clutching the steel in his pocket, ensuring that it hasn't fallen into the view of wide, innocent eyes.

The little girl is still staring as John scrambles for air, but the other man speaks to her calmly; tweaks his fingers through the gap in the wires in fond-hearted farewell.

"Run along and play now, sweetheart," he prods gently as she gapes at the stranger. "It's all right; I'll see you in a couple of hours."

She darts swiftly away, rejoining her friends in a lightning flash of bubble-gum pink, her pleated purple skirt flopping carelessly about thin tighted legs, the dangerous invader already forgotten.

The other man turns, gazes steadily at John, still hoarse and harassed, but now facing, himself, the youthful frenzy unfolding in fragments beyond the vigilant wire.

"Which one's yours?" the other man asks.

John inhales a ragged breath with which to speak. "The blond boy. On the swings. In the blue shirt. Matthew."

The child is pumping his legs awkwardly, struggling to work it, but smiling delightedly nonetheless, as if he's already in flight. "I'm Mark," the man replies, holding out a firm hand for John to shake. "And that's Sara," he adds, nodding towards the child jumping distractedly about the hopscotch board with two other small girls.

"John." John grips the extended hand, inspects its owner's genial green eyes, and wonders whether he ought to suspect them instead. "I haven't seen you here before."

"It's my first time," Mark admits. "I'm sure you heard... after what happened yesterday..."

Reluctantly John nods, his eyes trailing away across the schoolyard, the wide-open playground his son will cherish in the forthcoming years, the fragile brick building in which he will do most of his childhood learning and growing.

"How long have you been coming?" Mark inquires curiously.

"Since school started," John confides, his voice breaking as he tries not to think back on the long lonely hours spent at the edge of the fence, the long frigid ones that will soon be upon him; concentrates instead on the fierce joy that fills his heart each day when his son emerges, runs into his arms whole and unharmed.

Mark squints at the teachers gathering the children back into lines, into an order that defines and protects; fidgets with the twirl of wire topping the fence as his daughter breaks formation to raise two fingers in a tiny, clandestine wave. John, too, follows the now-familiar parade with haunted eyes: the teachers counting the glowing faces, searching nervously about in the pale autumn sunshine, shielding their charges from dangers unseen but no longer unknown.

"It's nice to know there's another," Mark interjects unexpectedly, scattering John's thoughts, recalling him to his duty as the children commence their stiff march back to their classrooms. Prompts him into a sullen, steady scan of the world surrounding the schoolyard, a world now threatening its peace, its innocence, its incipient beauty.

"Another?" John inquires vaguely, his thoughts lost amongst the wavering shadows lining the street and sidewalk, shadows that might conceal an enemy, perhaps even a friend.

"Guarding the perimeter, I mean," Mark explains, following John's gaze with his own dauntless, appraising eyes; doubling its power.

John stares searchingly at his fellow, who stares unflinching, searchingly back; two hunters in pursuit of the same prey. He nods again, brusquely, as he sweeps the last of the drying perspiration from his brow; focuses his eyes once more on the tow-headed boy glancing timidly over his shoulder and then reluctantly retreating beyond his sight. "It's a big perimeter."

He rattles the low fence as he strides back to his station, grips its coils lightly with the flexing fingers of one hand as he strokes the cold steel in his pocket with the other. A relentless watcher prowling the schoolyard, seeking the stranger, the savage, the psychotic stalking his little boy, Mark's little girl, any parent's little child. Grimly determined to keep watch, one day, one week, one year at a time; to keep childhood safe for children and wondrous for adults; to keep his child a child.

FLUFFY ROBES AND SLIPPERS

"Are you cold?" he inquired suspiciously.

"Of course not," she answered. "I'm wearing my big fluffy robe and slippers."

"They're ratty," he sniffed.

"They're comfy," she corrected him.

It was too much to bear. Here he had this lovely young wife, and she was continually shuffling around the house in that oversized fleece and furry footwear, even when they had guests.

"Listen, bub," she would say. "If you're going to invite your buddies over for a beer at eleven o'clock at night, you're darn right I'm going to meet them in my robe and slippers."

He pleaded and whined and cajoled, and at last they compromised. He would stop leaving his beard hairs in the bathroom sink if she would refrain from wearing the robe in front of company.

That had been many years ago, many robes and slippers ago, and now when he gazed at her lying prone on the bed that they shared, no longer a pretty young woman but a beautiful old one, he could hardly imagine her in any other outfit. It spoke to him of warm feet and cool hands, of the sheets that they had defrosted together, of the cozy softness of her front-door farewell on chill autumn mornings.

"Who's coming tonight, honey?" she inquired, her voice muffled by the curves of cushioned cloth tucked gently about her face and neck.

"Everyone!" he answered cheerfully, rearranging the flowers that stood in the vase by her bedside. "Kids, grandkids, your sister, your best friend…"

She was quiet a long moment. "You might have to help me change, sweetheart. I'm not feeling my best, you know."

"Nah," he said, pushing the machine by the bed aside and drawing a thick blanket up over her fragile frame. "I think for tonight you can be comfy."

This piece was the result of one of the very rare occasions in which I've been inspired to write a story by random brainstorming. It was winter, and I was standing in front of the kitchen sink washing dishes and trying to come up with an idea for an ultra-short, and not having very much success, I'm afraid. Then I looked down and saw that I was wearing… Well, I suppose you can guess what I was wearing.

This story was actually published on Thanksgiving Day here in the U.S., and I'll admit that at first I wasn't terribly pleased when I saw the schedule – I feared that people would naturally misread it as a Thanksgiving story, which, of course, was not my intention in writing it.

But then I thought, well, maybe it isn't such a stretch, at that. Perhaps there is an element of gratitude, of appreciation for one's loved ones; for the warmth and ceaseless devotion of one's family and friends. How often do people who are on the verge of extinction long for just one more Christmas, one more birthday, yes, even one more Thanksgiving with those they love best? How often, too, are they most sorely missed and most fondly remembered on those very occasions, those special times in which our attention is particularly drawn to the people whose lives we have shared?

Maybe, in some small way, my story was about Thanksgiving after all.

THE AUTOCRAT

He hacked. It was coming in gushes now, the blood in his sputum, the cureless calamity of his body and soul.

"Name a successor," his adviser had urged, on reviewing the doctor's report. Secretly hoping, perhaps, that it would be he.

It wouldn't be. The Minister had no son; no child to carry on when he was gone. No reason to carry on at all.

The years of service had exhausted him. Few understood it, the strain of monocracy. His subjects perceived only its magnificence: the fine clothes, the luxurious automobiles, the sumptuous banquets with world-renowned guests. They could not guess at the responsibility that accompanied it, the knowledge that he was ultimately accountable for every decision, every difficulty of the people. When they loved, it was him that they loved. But when they despised...

He coughed again, spat into the bronze basin, and watched the discolored mucus slide slowly out of sight, leaving a watery crimson trail behind it. It was nearly time.

He roused, rose from his crouch and straightened with effort. Plastered on an expression of confidence, of disdain for the concern of his aides and staff; prepared to traverse the narrow corridor to the elevator, to descend to the clandestine chamber where he would make his final arrangements.

He walked. Strolled, even, a man without cares, a well-faked smile playing upon his lips. "Good morning, gentlemen. Lovely weather today." Cleared his throat casually, swallowed and tasted blood. But kept walking.

The guards didn't pause, but parted at once before him, politely permitting him to punch the keypad. His orders were unquestioned, unquestionable. Even in that room his motives lay beyond suspicion.

He settled on the big chair at the wide table, flipped a switch and waited as its cover rolled back like a convertible readying itself for a smooth Sunday drive. Revealed dozens of multi-colored motorists sitting cheerfully inside, eagerly anticipating being pointed in their assigned directions.

He made his selections carefully, consulting the map with its pinpricks of populace, of dense cities and sparse countrysides. He'd known already, of course, what his primary choices would be, but he was determined to ensure evenness, a flawless distribution. That there might be no error, no leak, no gap in the storm or the winter to follow. No chance for anything less than totality, completion.

He hacked again. Expelled the bloody mass out onto the floor and left it where it fell. Examined it bemusedly, sensible to its meaning but detached from its portent. Acquiesced to the death that it represented, the certain death that even now was haunting his steps, blocking his path.

He smiled. It certainly was easier this way. It was much less unpleasant to go knowing that everyone else was going to go, too.

A twitch of his finger and the program began. Yes. Code. Yes. Another code. Yes, code, yes. Confirmed. Done.

He leaned back in the captain's chair. Felt the rumbling

overhead and laughed; reclined and relaxed as the people, the nation, the world ended without him.

OVERPASS

It stretched loftily above; an iron-gray arch sweeping skyward and high. She remembered back to when they'd built it, the new entrance with its promise of escape, a mid-city launching point onto the wide highway that snaked its way towards everywhere, anywhere. A delusion hardened into cold steel and concrete.

Joe hadn't been able to take it. Sam had watched him rise in the early moonlight hours and go. Had lain awake awaiting his return, which didn't come.

His pacing on the rough gravel had troubled her sleep; woken her.

"What's up, Sam?" she'd yawned.

"Go back to sleep, kid," he'd answered gruffly. He answered everything gruffly. "Joe went for a walk; he'll be back soon."

But Gina knew that couldn't be true or Sam wouldn't be pacing. She'd gotten up; waited with him. Waited and watched, the empty old road, the tattered train tracks, the barren night sky. At last spotted the shadow, the form leaning over the edge of the railing far overhead. And screamed without thinking, rousing the whole camp at once.

"Don't do it, Joe," Sam called. "That's one mistake you can't ever erase."

"C'mon down, Joe," Bob shouted. "It'll get better, you'll see. You gotta give it more time."

Joe wavered almost imperceptibly, hesitating, perhaps, in the face of so many witnesses to his fall, his failure.

"The girl's right here, Joe," Sam hollered again. "You really gonna do this in front of her?"

Gina resented it, the implication that she wasn't tough; was too delicate to watch a man splatter himself all over the sidewalk. But still she didn't want to see it.

"You'll get us all kicked out!" Martin had yelled with sudden inspiration. "Put us all out onto the street. Don't do that to us, Joe!"

And that had settled it. Joe couldn't, wouldn't betray their fellowship, their community. He'd vanished from the guardrail and returned to camp interminable minutes later, shaky but intact. He'd gratefully accepted the pint they'd all chipped in for with their quarters and dimes; they'd sent her to the late-night store around the corner to fetch it. It hadn't occurred to the clerk that she might be too young to purchase a bottle of liquor. It never did.

It hadn't lasted, though. Three weeks later Joe went for a walk again and never returned. They heard the ambulance and police sirens screeching on the overpass in the middle of rush hour and Sam had hurried down the block and up the stone walkway to look. Sidled quietly towards the accident site; saw the car smashed up onto the sidewalk, the weeping driver, the covered stretcher. And a single shabby shoe, its laces gone, its rubber worn through.

She'd displayed it on a concrete block in the center of camp, in remembrance of Joe. But it made them all look anxiously at their own feet, their own filthy, holey socks, their own shoes worn through to the skin. Soles worn out by asphalt and pavement. Souls worn out beneath a stony-faced overpass.

SQUIRREL REVOLUTION

I actually had the idea that sparked this story a number of years ago. I don't recall how I came up with it exactly, but one day I started thinking about the evolutionary process and how it relates to the impact of man on the environment. There's no doubt that humans are greatly, if not solely, responsible for the extinction of a large number of species, hunting and habitat destruction being two of the primary means by which animal and plant life have gravely diminished in a world in which humans have become predominant. However, if there's one thing that evolutionary theory teaches us, it's that life is incredibly adaptable. Remember learning in school about the changes that took place in the moth population during the Industrial Revolution in England? Within a very short space of time the predominantly white moth population became a predominantly black one – because moths had a greater chance of survival when they were better able to blend in with their new, sootier environment. And they reproduce quickly enough to put those physical adaptations in place in the blink of a human eye.

So it seems reasonable to suppose that similar changes would occur in other species whose environments have been severely impacted by human activities. Indeed, it may be those species that are best able to adapt to a human-dominated landscape that will continue to thrive into the next century. The ant. The cockroach. The pigeon. The squirrel.

I think it would make for an interesting scientific study, if anyone were sufficiently motivated to do it, to monitor the world's population of squirrels and track whether they've adopted physical or cognitive adaptations in response to alterations in their environment. We think we know how squirrels behave. We see them running halfway across the street and then suddenly scurrying back when they see a car coming, which is how they get hit half the time. But what about the ones we don't see, the ones who are too smart or too nimble to get caught in traffic? What if there really is something else going on behind the scenes? Look out! It's a Squirrel Revolution!

Sheriff Wiggins scowled and hung up the phone with a bang and a sigh.

"What is it, Sherriff?" his scrawny young deputy Sam inquired automatically, gazing dreamily out the window as if his thoughts were roaming among the tree-lined streets of the town.

"Pete Grundy says he saw a funny-lookin' squirrel," the Sheriff answered.

The deputy guffawed, his attention abruptly reclaimed. "A squirrel?"

"A squirrel," Wiggins affirmed. "Claims he saw it run and then jump clear across Old Logjam Road, from one side to the other, without touchin' ground."

"That ol' Pete," Sam smiled, chuckling and shaking his head as if reality really was sometimes more amusing than dreams.

"Come on," the Sheriff ordered. "We're goin' to check

it out."

"Why, Sheriff!" Sam answered in disbelief. "You know Grundy shoots whiskey daily startin' at noon."

"Sure 'nough. But it's only nine," the Sheriff replied, angling his clean-shaven chin towards the clock on the wall.

"Since when do we concern ourselves with critters like squirrels?" the deputy demanded suspiciously, his eyes narrowing like a magnifying glass attempting to focus a beam of sunshine into a ray of kindling fire.

"Since Grundy asked me to, and since I owe him a favor," Wiggins replied flatly, his manner clearly indicating that the discussion was closed, leaving Sam to wonder under what circumstances and in what capacity the Sheriff had found himself in the debt of the town drunk. "Besides," he added, in somewhat conciliatory fashion, "I been meaning to set up a speed trap on that road for a while anyhow; it won't hurt us none to keep our eyes open while we're out there."

Their watchful eyes nabbed numerous speeders, but no peculiar squirrels, only the rather ordinary ones who rushed heedlessly across the highway in an effort to evade the vehicles which, resplendent and rickety alike, cruised recklessly around the curves of the road as if it were their own private racecourse. When the daylight at last began to dim underneath the generous canopy of trees, and suppertime was drawing near, Wiggins decided to collect his antsy-pantsed deputy and call it a day. Sam had wandered off a little ways into the wood; was taking a leak at the base of a tough-looking shrub when the Sheriff heard him calling softly, "Come and take a look at this, Sheriff."

Wiggins snorted, stamping his foot impatiently. "You got nothing there I want to see."

"Not that!" Sam replied in a huff, hastily zipping up his trousers. "There's a funny creature over here."

At that, the Sheriff stepped over the guardrail and strode the dozen paces into the wood to join his befuddled deputy. Squatting on the ground not ten feet in front of them, staring intently at the strangers, was a bushy-tailed brown squirrel. The Sheriff nearly scoffed; made ready to call Sam a fool for having a conniption over a common squirrel, when he, too, noticed that there was something strange about it. Its face was all wrong. Its eyes weren't off to the side, but on the front of its head, like a cat or a dog. And it didn't look at you like a squirrel normally did either, the way their eyes never seemed to focus on anything, but more like a larger animal might, as if it recognized you for what you were.

The Sheriff and his deputy both stood gaping for a time at the oddly formed creature, until at last, evidently becoming bored with the contest it had so obviously won, it bounded nonchalantly away, leaving the two men standing dubiously dumbstruck at the edge of the darkening forest. Finally Wiggins nodded to himself as if in affirmation and said, "Let's go," to Sam, who at once hurried toward their waiting cruiser and its reassuring promise of punctual homecoming.

Wiggins had just cranked the engine when the whoosh of rubber rolling rapidly over asphalt assaulted their ears from around the bend right behind them, forewarning them that another speeder was approaching. Tensely they waited in anticipation of the day's last catch, Sam quickly raising the radar gun to clock the offender. But when the unfamiliar sedan flew past them in a flurry of dead leaves and loose pebbles, the Sheriff didn't punch the gas, but instead sat gazing at the road in an apparent stupor until Sam elbowed him in the arm.

"Come on, Sheriff, don't you wanna nab that guy?" Sam prodded anxiously, perplexed by this unnatural ruffling of the Sheriff's usual unbreakably calm demeanor. "Looked like an out-of-towner, even!"

Wiggins paused before speaking, removing his hat and running his fingers distractedly through the fine bristles that lined his short-shaven head. "Thought I saw something," he said finally, reaching for his holster and stroking it as if for reassurance. "Flyin' up over the road as that car went by. Like a small animal jumping. Jumpin' on awfully big legs."

The Sheriff spent most of the following day on the old-fashioned telephone at the stationhouse, playing unmusical tunes with its big square buttons while he scratched notes and doodles in the margins of his giant desk calendar. Who did you call about deformed squirrels? Luckily he had a buddy in the capital, who, with no small reservations, cleared him to talk to his buddy at the capital who might know something about someone who might know someone he could maybe talk to about it. Sam's amusement with this prolonged process had wilted by late morning, and by mid-afternoon, he was heartily bored.

"Come on, Sheriff," he whined, peeling the chipped ivory paint from the windowsill while Wiggins sat fiddling with the phone cord, on a seemingly interminable hold for the nineteenth time that day. "Let's do somethin', huh? What makes you think anybody cares about the squirrels around here, anyway?"

The Sheriff silenced him with one finger as the phone burst briefly into life. A moment later he was holding his hand over the mouthpiece and gloating, "Washington cares, that's who. They're connecting me now."

Sam listened with greater interest while the Sheriff recounted the story of the two squirrels to the party in

Washington, wondering if they had already sent for those men in the white coats to fetch his boss when the call was over. But the conversation seemed peaceable enough, and the Sheriff satisfied as he concluded, "Yes, I sure will do that. Yes, I've got the number. Thank you, sir." He returned the big plastic receiver to its proper place, rubbing his ear in discomfort as he did so, and then tilted back in his chair and gazed thoughtfully out the window that Sam had so lately been denuding while the deputy fidgeted in his boots, awaiting an explanation.

"Well, what did they say?!" he finally exploded, when none was forthcoming.

The Sheriff didn't answer, but merely continued tilting back in his chair, and then leaning it forward, and then back again while the floorboards creaked irritably beneath his shifting weight.

"How much do you know about evolution, Sam?" he said at length, bringing the chair to a halt and at last giving the flooring a rest.

Sam shrugged. "Not much," he admitted.

"Well, I learned about it in college," Wiggins replied casually.

"You mean in those two years you were at State?" Sam scoffed.

"Those two years is what made me a Sheriff, and you a deputy," Wiggins answered scathingly, causing Sam to cringe and blush. "Matter of fact, I learned all manner of useful things in those two years. See, every so often in nature there's a mistake called a genetic mutation. Most of 'em are bad, but every so often they're advantageous to the creatures that get 'em, and they have lots of babies and pass those traits on to all their children. You know, like with giraffes. The ones with long necks could get better food, so nature kept favorin' ones with long necks until they grew into what you see today. Get it?"

Sam nodded, his self-esteem blissfully restored.

"Well, what do you suppose might happen if there were somethin' in a creature's environment that was real dangerous? Maybe it's a deadly disease; people who were naturally immune to that sickness would outlive the others, wouldn't they? And then pass their genes on to their kin, making them immune, too?" Sam nodded again, thinking that maybe you did learn some pretty interesting things in college after all. "An' if the disease was bad enough, and widespread enough, eventually only the people who were immune to it might be left. Now what do you suppose is the most dangerous thing in the world to a squirrel?"

Sam thought a moment, scratching his skinny thigh nervously with spindly fingers before his face lit up in comprehension. "Rabies!"

"Well, that's not a bad answer," the Sheriff conceded. "But most often you don't find 'em dead from rabies, do you? You find 'em dead…"

"…on the road," the deputy finished the sentence, face glimmering with the hope that he finally understood the point of the Sheriff's protracted speech. "So a squirrel that grew big legs could jump high over a road and wouldn't get hit by cars."

"Exactly!" Wiggins replied. "And you know what else? I been thinkin' 'bout that other funny squirrel we saw, the one with eyes up here, that looked right at you?" he said, gesturing towards his own steely grays. "See, that ain't natural for a squirrel. A squirrel is a prey animal; I mean, other creatures eat it. And normally a prey animal has eyes on the sides of its head, so it can see all around it, like, and tell if somethin's comin' after it. Predatory animals, like a wolf or a lion, they got eyes more facing forward; they get better depth perception that way, which makes 'em better hunters. So if a squirrel's got eyes in the front of his head, I can only think of two reasons for it. One, it helps him figure out how close cars are, and how fast they're comin', so he knows whether it's safe to cross the street or not."

"You always see 'em runnin' back and forth, like they can't decide!" Sam interjected excitedly.

"That's exactly right, an' that's how a lot of 'em get hit. They start goin' and then stop." He paused. "The other possibility is that maybe the squirrels are learnin' to hunt."

"That'd sure be a sight," the deputy said with wonder.

"It sure would," Wiggins replied, gazing out the window again in troubled contemplation, as if wondering whether, even now, a giant squirrel with big teeth and a bigger appetite was approaching their small and poorly defended shack.

"But wait a minute, Sheriff!" Sam exclaimed after a thoughtful moment, tearing the Sheriff away from his disturbing fantasy. "What did Washington say about it?"

Sheriff Wiggins waved his hand dismissively. "They said they were trained squirrels of a different breed from some travelling Russian circus. Said a bunch of 'em escaped into the wild, and that it was nothing to worry about."

Sam resumed his struggle to comprehend the Sheriff's complacency, scratching his leg even more vigorously before moving on to his hairless chest. "But if that's all it is, then what's the big deal? They're just foreign squirrels."

"The big deal, Sam," the Sheriff replied, his steely eyes glinting, "Is that they told me to call again if I saw any more like it. Now when did anybody in Washington tell you to call them again unless it was somethin' really serious? Russian squirrels, my ass. I'd sooner believe that ol' Pete Grundy went on the wagon."

***

Agent Matthews scowled and hung up the phone with a bang and a sigh. "There's been another sighting," she said gruffly to her colleague, who was intently scrutinizing a complicated computer graph at the desk beside hers.

"Where?" Collins answered, creasing his eyebrows into an arch that wiggled like the lines connecting the plot points he was examining so closely.

Matthews slapped a spot on the map that hung on the wall beside her, frowning as if she found it irritating or even offensive.

"That means it's spreading," Collins declared unnecessarily, glancing back at his graph and its dancing maze of circles and arcs. "Almost every state now. What kind was it?"

"Them," Matthews corrected him, pressing her temples as if to stave off an impending headache. "The jumper and the one with the funny eyes."

"Both in one place? That's odd."

"The Sheriff who called said it was on a busy rural thoroughfare. Everyone in town takes it as a shortcut to the next town over. He'd set up a speed trap on it."

"Sounds conducive to both varieties, then." Then, dropping his voice to a troubled whisper, Collins inquired, "No more of that other kind yet, are there?"

"Not yet," Matthews replied in an equally hushed tone, discreetly leaning towards her partner as if confiding a top secret. "Speaking of which, we should head up to the test site before the trials are over."

It was short ride on the elevator from the orderly cube of fluorescent-lit underground offices to the dim, thickly-forested surface where the site had been constructed. A man in a loose, long-sleeved lab coat stood hunched over a clipboard taking notes. He was wearing violet earplugs, presumably to cut the loud rumble of motors that echoed like a pride of full-grown lions chasing a fleeing gazelle. But when he saw Matthews and Collins approaching, he signaled for a stoppage, and the two sedans, two pickup trucks, and two motorcycles that had been revolving in great loops around them shuddered to a halt.

"Did you get him yet?" Collins queried.

The operator consulted his notes. "Eight times. At least once with each vehicle."

"And?"

"No effect," he smiled with obvious admiration.

"Where is it now?" Matthews inquired, scrunching up her nose as if trying to pick up its scent.

"On the inside, at the west end."

The agents lifted their binoculars and directed their gazes accordingly. The test site was an oval track, constructed of thick asphalt and built in the midst of a dense wood that had been domed and walled round about to keep out curiosity-seekers who might venture this far into the forest. Even as they watched from their vantage point in the center, they observed the crane dumping the pile of acorns on the outside of the track, while the various vehicles resumed their ceaseless race around it. In a few moments, a bold squirrel emerged snuffling at the edge of the wood, evidently smelling the nuts across the way, and sprinted across the road just as one of the pickups was approaching. All three of the observers flinched as the furry animal was brutally crushed under the truck's heavy tires, its body toppling backwards in the windy wake of the two-ton machine. But even before the vehicle had rounded the next bend, the squirrel had shaken itself and was on its feet again, resuming its race to the other side of the road as if it had merely lost its footing.

"Remarkable!" the man-in-charge exclaimed as they watched a heavy metal cage plop precipitously down on the animal as it frisked about the pile of acorns it had mastered through its desperate courage.

"I still can't believe that it could… that it could function like that," Matthews said with awe, slapping her fingers against her forehead as if trying to force her brain to comprehend what was happening.

"It is incredible," the supervisor agreed. "But not entirely without precedent. Didn't you ever have a hamster as a child? Those creatures can flatten their bodies enough to crawl underneath a door."

"But this…!" Matthews interjected, wiping her sweat-fogged glasses with her blouse. "This is an extreme adaptation, isn't it?"

"Extreme circumstances produce extreme measures," the supervisor theorized with affected superiority. "What manner of animal survived following the asteroid which drove the dinosaurs to extinction? Small furry mammals; ratlike creatures. And what is a squirrel but a glorified rat?"

He smiled complacently and went back to his notes as Collins and Matthews turned to go. But halfway to the elevator they heard muffled yelling and looked back to find the supervisor frantically waving his arms in order to catch their attention. "Wait, I nearly forgot!" he shouted over the noise of cars that was again resonating throughout the dome. "The litter that she bore last week. It seems that she's passed it on."

The agents gaped, their mouths hanging open like ill-conceived flytraps. "The offspring are the same?"

"It appears so, now that they have grown. But they would have to be, anyway, to have survived in the womb during the trials, wouldn't you think?" Again he smiled broadly, as if pleased with the impressive accomplishments of his subject of study, while the agents retreated towards the elevator.

The following week, Matthews and Collins were still puzzling over the data from the track when another call came in from Sheriff Wiggins.

"Yes, Sheriff," Matthews answered breathlessly. "Have you seen any more of those odd squirrels?"

"No, not those," the Sheriff responded. "But a real funny thing happened night before last. You see, I got a call from Ol' Lady Teasdale asking me to come out 'cause she'd run over a squirrel. Squished it good, she said. Now if it were anyone else, I'd tell 'em to go hang, but she's a dear, tenderhearted thing – the kind that calls the fire department to fetch a cat out of a tree – and she was real upset, cryin' and all 'cause she'd hurt a poor defenseless creature, so I said I'd go."

Wiggins paused to take a deep breath while Collins and Matthews bent over the telephone like children preparing to bob for apples. "Now here's the strange part. When I got there, it turned out she hadn't exactly run over the squirrel; it was more like she had parked on top of it. And she was jes' standin' there starin' down at it lyin' quietly under the wheel, so I says to her, 'Well, I don't see that there's much we can do about it now 'scept give it a decent burial. If you'll be so kind as to lend me your keys, Ma'am, I'll, uh, release it and set free its heavenly soul.' And that makes her stop cryin' so she hands over the keys and I get in the car and reverse it a couple of feet, and Ol' Lady Teasdale starts screaming so loud I think I've run over her foot so I stop the car and jump out.

"When I get to her, she don't look hurt, but she's still hysterical, shouting, 'It's a miracle, Sheriff, a miracle! Call the pastor!'

" 'Wait a minute now,' I said, 'The pastor's probably busy workin' out his sermon for tomorrow, so let's not disturb him unless we're sure we got to – what miracle are you talkin' 'bout here?'

" 'The squirrel, Sheriff! It just jumped up and ran away, not even hurt.'

"An' I looked down and sure enough, that squirrel was nowhere to be seen. I checked the ground an' I checked the car an' I checked all around the yard an' I even checked the bottom of the old lady's shoes but that squirrel weren't nowhere. And the weird thing is that I know I saw it flattened there under that wheel, and, as a matter of fact, I pulled out a little tuft o' grayish-brown hair from her tire, which proved we weren't both seein' things. I even searched the driveway for a hole that it mighta been layin' in, but there wasn't one, and her tires were solid, too. And I jes' plumb can't understand how a simple ol' squirrel could survive that kind of crushing unless it had like, a rubber skeleton, or organs that could flatten themselves, or move out of the way when they wanted to, or somethin' sophisticated an' unnatural like that."

Matthews and Collins examined one another searchingly. "Well, naturally that's ridiculous," Matthews said shakily into the speakerphone, her voice barely inclining to a whisper. "There must be some other explanation. A rational one," she added hastily.

"Well, I am sure glad to hear you say that, Ma'am," Wiggins replied with feeling. "Because I tell you what, I'd be darn scared of a squirrel that had eyes like a wildcat, could leap over a two-lane highway in one jump, and not even be injured by a ton of metal lyin' plumb on top of it. With as quick as they make babies, creatures like that would overrun the country in no time," he concluded sagely.

"We appreciate your call," Collins snapped, cutting off Matthews, who was on the verge of agreeing with the Sheriff. "Call us again with any other news."

The clash of the phone being reinserted into its base

rang out in the comparative silence that followed.

"I think maybe you were right," Collins said slowly, after a long pause. "Nothing else we've tried so far has worked. Maybe there is something to be done with the owls."

"Everybody likes owls!" Matthews exclaimed hopefully. "But if they evolve to catch the super-squirrels, won't they become like, super-owls?"

"That's a chance we'll have to take," Collins answered grimly.

"Just imagine..." Matthews said faintly, almost dreamily, "All this, a result of people driving automobiles. Automobiles driving evolution!"

And back at his office, Sheriff Wiggins was installing bars on the window of the stationhouse and saying to his deputy, "I don't care what you call it, Sam. God, Nature, evolution... it sure does work in mysterious ways."

BEACH HOUSE

Dawn came, as warm and welcoming as the weathered beach house in which she lay so peacefully snoozing. The tickling rays of the sun trickled in through the bare wood-framed window, caressing her cheek and kissing her brow as if tucking her in for a restful night's sleep. The waves rocked tranquilly outside: a sweet, serenading lullaby to lull the listener into soft slumber and gentle dreams.

Then a seagull shrieked by the window and she woke with a start to a bright, beautiful morning; a brilliant azure sky that perfectly matched the blue of her sweetheart's eyes.

Susan rose, pressed her feet gingerly against the cool floorboards and tiptoed noiselessly down the hall, as if fearful of waking someone. In the foyer she stopped and studied her reflection in a vast decorative mirror lining the wall. And then turned to the door and opened it wide, as wide as the welcoming arms with which she intended to greet him.

The stoop was empty, as she had known it would be.

She sighed. He wasn't coming. She had told him not to. That, to her, was love.

She retreated to the kitchen to make her coffee. She sipped at it while she re-read Derek's old-fashioned handwritten letter, the ink wandering in curlicues gently across the page like the bubbling bits of foam that trailed across the sand at the edge of the ocean outside their door. She wondered if he, too, was sitting in their city apartment that morning re-reading the answer she had sent him last week.

"Please don't come, darling. I want your last memories of the beach house to be wonderful, joyful ones. I want us both to remember how it was, how happy we were, before this happened. I love you too much to let you see me this way."

She rose resolutely and returned to the bedroom to dress.

Half an hour later she emerged into the magnificent morning, her heart as light as her step as she propelled her thin body across the rough sand, her toes delighting in the warmth of the granules that crept up between them, her eyes dazzled by the beauty of the sun on the water. Off in the distance it beckoned, the rocky point to which she and Derek had so often walked on glorious days like these, running gaily from the waves that slapped their ankles and then unexpectedly splashed their thighs; holding hands as if they were one creature, one being, one soul. A creature no longer divisible into two separate beings; a soul that sang with one rhythm, one chord.

A cloud settled on the horizon, and the world dimmed and faded. Still she walked, her pulse, her breath quickened by the exercise. Her step wavered but she steadied herself, dreaming of Derek, of their casual sunset strolls, their romantic picnics on the sand. The wind picked up and she faltered but pressed on, her legs growing as heavy as the sky now darkening with clouds and unfallen rain. The promontory was still a distant speck; barely, it seemed, had she progressed away from the house, which stood now so inviting with its promise of relaxation and rest. She turned back, panicking, and roughly inhaled the cool wind that whipped the shoreline, ruffling the feathers of the seabirds that cringed in the face of the oncoming storm. The salty air clung thickly to her skin as she trudged back along the beach, her hair fluttering in disarray about her neck and shoulders, gritty grains of sand assaulting her eyes, her nose, her mouth. Gasping, she halted, grimacing with pain, while the first drops flew fiercely around her, plummeting into the spray and the sand and the soft skin of her scalp like tiny bullets that pierced and destroyed. Hopeless, she surrendered; crumpled at last to her knees while the rain crashed around her, waiting for the pain to subside and contemplating the doctor's bleak words, so compassionately delivered, so helplessly received.

"Won't I at least have the summer?" she had inquired, still half full of hope; half full of the promise of the few wonderful months that she and Derek might still joyfully share.

"You'll need constant bedrest," he'd informed her quietly, shaking his head. "Any exertion could bring it on that much sooner. And you'd be better off being in the hospital. I'm afraid it will be very… painful, near the end."

She buried her face in her hands and thought again of Derek, of the countless happy moments they had shared here together, of the moments she would miss without him by her side. Almost she thought she could feel his strong arms entwining around her, feel her spirit lifting as he raised her, then carried her laughing over the threshold as he did every summer, as if he were her groom and she his new bride.

"No, Susan," a voice whispered as a strong hand brushed a lock of wet hair from her cheek and soft lips pressed tenderly against the lines of her forehead.

She removed her hands from her face and opened her

eyes. Derek gazed lovingly back at her, his eyes as blue as the sky that was again clearing above them.

"I want to be with you, Susan," he said. "I love you too much to leave you alone." He hoisted her thin body in his arms and stood, his face glowing in the brightening light.

"This is how I want to remember the beach house," he said, his deep voice breaking. "This is how I want to remember you. Lying in my arms, every night and every morning, every day until the end."

He drew her closer and began walking, with her in his arms, back to the house.

Susan looked up. The clouds had gone. The waves lapped gently at the shore. And over their heads, the sun shone.

She smiled. Never would she walk alone. This, then, was love. Having someone to walk with you to the end. Whenever it comes.

I'll be the first to admit that this is a pretty sad story for a romance, but compared to the first version I wrote, this one's all flowers and rainbows!

I originally wrote this piece in response to a contest prompt. Stories for the contest were supposed to feature a weathered beach house and a woman placing a key in an envelope. I confess I had quite a bit of trouble coming up with a storyline, and when I finally did, it was a doozy. The basis of the story was essentially the same as in the second version you read above, except that Susan actually is expecting Derek to arrive. However, in order to incorporate the element of the key and the suggested wording, I had to take drastic measures. This was the original (now the alternate) ending:

"The storm had passed when at last she arose; vanished into the house and emerged many minutes later wearing a clean, dry sundress and carrying a light backpack; a weary traveler yearning for rest. Struggling her way over to her favorite spot on the porch, she sat; took two pills from an orange bottle clenched in her fist and swallowed them whole. She tucked the bottle into her bag and then fumbled through its contents until she retrieved a pen and a crisp envelope creased neatly in half. Awkwardly she unfolded it; opened the flap and dropped a shining silver key inside it; the key to the oceanside home that they had once so happily shared. With trembling fingers, she inscribed the stiff white paper with six simple words and left them there for him to read; for him to try to understand.

Sometimes it does hurt to hope.

Hoisting her bag upon frail, fallen shoulders, she tripped clumsily away from the weathered beach house and across the weather-beaten sand, no longer having a point or a destination. No longer having a companion, to walk with her across the beach to the end."

Now that is a sad story.

Besides being incredibly depressing, that version somehow never felt right to me, but I couldn't figure out a good way to fix it. Finally I had the bright idea of giving it a happy(ish) ending, and voila – it became my third piece to be featured in *Romance Flash*.

NIGHT FALLS

"But I don't like explosives!" Joan insisted, twisting her fingers through her long, filthy hair.

"What explosives?" Tom countered with an irritated sigh. "It's just a model rocket!"

The broken-gated entrance to the abandoned quarry loomed before them, silhouetted against the evening sky like a forgotten sentinel still gravely guarding a once-precious gem. Tom swerved suddenly towards it, crashing the car over a ridge in the road and sending them flying close to the edge of the pit of half-unearthed stones.

"Watch it!" Joan cried, but Tom was already leaping out and seeking a clearing for the launch site.

"C'mon, it'll be dark soon!" he exclaimed, tearing the cellophane from a fresh box of matches and raising one in his clenched fist, his face glowing in the kindling fire.

With the ferocity of a tiny jet engine, the rocket exploded into the darkening dusk and utterly vanished from sight.

"That's strange," Tom said after a minute, staring skyward after the still-absent envoy to the heavens. "It should have come down by now."

All at once, the sky seemed to bow overhead, caving in towards them as if warped by forces unseen or unknown, while the stars that had peacefully accented its once-immutable face bent threateningly down upon the clearing where they cowered agape.

"You broke it!" Joan accused as the atmosphere thickened, scattering the earth beneath their feet and sending the remaining rocks tumbling into the depths of the pit. "You and your explosives!"

Tom merely stood and watched in awe as the night finally fell.

I wrote this short-short for Flash Fiction Chronicles' "String of 10" Contest. The premise of the contest is a list of ten randomly generated words and a suggestive theme. You're supposed to use at least four of the words and your interpretation of the theme to create a story of no more than 250 words. Here was the prompt:

Evening – Quarry – Accent – Rose – Tear – Minute – Grave – Close – Entrance – Bow

I want to put a ding in the universe. —Steve Jobs

I decided to use all ten words – I figured that was part of the challenge – and I interpreted the Steve Jobs quote quite literally. The result was "Night Falls," an interesting if somewhat bizarre little piece that's totally unlike anything else I've ever written. Guess that proves it – writing prompts really do provide creative inspiration!

POISONED

"Tell them what you gave me, sweetheart," she prompted encouragingly, referring, perhaps, to a pair of earrings, a bouquet of flowers.

"What I gave you?" he replied, puzzled.

Lately she often said and did things that he didn't understand. At first he'd thought it was nerves. She was anxious by nature, becoming agitated in heavy traffic, on dark corners, in shops that were crowded. When she'd refused to answer the door for the mail carrier, he'd supposed that she'd been spooked by one of those creepy documentary crime shows that she liked to watch.

"You know what I mean," she asserted, her glassy green eyes sliding over his.

"I'm afraid I don't." Utterly bewildered now, he leaned over to reach for her quaking hand and then withdrew when she retreated, balking at his touch.

He'd even been entertained when she'd begun naming those who might be coming for her.

"The president of the PTA wants to kill me," she had declared in a deadpan voice.

He'd chuckled. "And why would she want to do that?"

"Several years ago I made fun of a blouse she was wearing. She's never forgotten it."

The anecdote seemed less amusing now.

"Please, honey," she urged. "You won't get into any trouble. I'm not even angry. I'm sure you didn't really mean to hurt me. Just please tell them; tell them now, before it's too late."

He should have insisted, that day last week when he'd come home from work to find her punching holes in the kitchen ceiling with a tire iron.

"What the hell are you doing?!!" he'd cried, coughing as he inhaled a cloud of dust and insulation.

"My father's hiding in the crawlspace. I don't know what he's planning."

"Your father's dead, Sheila."

"I never saw his body. Did you? You know how he hated me. He always hated me."

And now they were here, confined to this sparkling white room, surrounded by the infernal flashing and beeping of ominous machinery. The culmination of the nightmare of today. The chest pains, the shortness of breath, the terrible headache, all seemingly without cause. A panic attack, he had suspected. Had diligently driven her to the hospital, just in case. But this...he hadn't expected this.

"I'm sorry, sweetheart," he answered at last, peering sadly into her hollow eyes. "I really don't know what you're talking about."

She sighed and let her head droop gently back upon the pillow, her scraggly chestnut hair splayed in disarray about her elongated face and neck.

After the kitchen incident, he'd gently suggested that she seek help. Mental help.

"Lots of people go to psychiatrists, honey," he'd reassured her. "I just hate to see you so worried all the time."

"I'll think it over, Tom," she'd replied with such sweet reasonableness that he'd let the matter drop, convinced that she'd come around of her own volition.

She was rousing again, as if in response to his thoughts; was leaning towards him, her eyes meeting his, suddenly blinking with tenderness, recognition of the man she called husband. She held out a single shivering hand, palm up and open, in gesture almost of believing, of welcome, of reaching out to him with hands and heart. "Tom," she said quietly, with feeling, and his heart leapt, and his hand, too, leapt forward to take hold of her, to pull her from the depths over which she was so precariously poised, to cling desperately, intently to her; mind, body and soul.

She jerked suddenly away; tore herself from the proffered handhold; grasped instead the wire secured to her chest. Slowly she turned to face her attendants. "He's not going to admit it, is he?" she mused dolefully, seeking pity in the eyes of the hovering physician, the wide-eyed nurse, and then lapsing into an exhausted, anguished, wide-awake dream.

Tom gazed longingly at her, the woman he had so lately loved, who had so lately loved him. Wept as she transformed before him, her eyes falling out of focus, no longer seeing the world around them but a hidden, more frightening one within. Watched his wife journey to a place where he could never join her, a place where she would live alone now; a place without him.

This was a tricky piece to put together. It was actually inspired by an incident that occurred in the course of my mother's psychosis. One day she took me to the hospital, complaining of chest and abdominal pains. I was naturally concerned, but I also recall being hopeful that having a doctor examine her would lead to the (I thought) inevitable revelation that she'd lost her marbles. No such luck. But they did take her complaints seriously, because although she was in fairly good health, at forty-one she wasn't exactly young anymore, and was a smoker besides, so there was legitimate reason to believe there could be a problem with her heart. They gave her the requisite battery of tests, but couldn't find anything wrong. Now, as an adult, I can guess what they must have told her – that she'd had an anxiety attack, which she probably had – but at the age of sixteen, of course, I had no idea such a thing even existed. In fact, as she was imagining a lot of strange things in those days, I was more inclined to believe that her heartache was all in her head. But then the doctor left the room and the interrogation began. And that's when I began to be afraid that she'd somehow manage to pin the blame for her mysterious illness on me.

The first version I wrote of this piece was mostly reflective of that – my terror over being falsely accused and probably convicted of poisoning my own mother with some mysterious substance of which no one could prove or disprove the existence. I sent my story off to *The Journal of Microliterature*, and a few weeks later I got a response back from the editor that basically said (politely) that I had ruined an otherwise good piece by changing the tone halfway through. He – or she, as the editor there prefers to maintain his or her anonymity – was absolutely right. The story ended in hysterics, with the husband being dragged away by the police, which, while it carried the plot in an interesting direction, utterly wrecked the dreadful calm of the first half of the story. He or she did, however, say that if I ever did a rewrite, I should feel free to resubmit the revision.

So I rewrote it. I changed the second half of the piece entirely, including the ending, making it more about the relationship between the husband and wife than about the consequences of the wife's accusation. And I was careful to maintain the tone of the first half of the piece throughout, which worked worlds better than the original version. And here you see the results. How grateful I am to that editor! With one brief sentence he or she nailed what was wrong with that piece and clued me in as to how to change it from a so-so story into a well-done one. I realize, of course, that few editors have the time to address the defects in the submissions they receive. But I hope that those who do make the effort are aware of how much we writers truly appreciate their feedback, and of what an impact a few choice words can make on our quality of work.

STATE OF MICRONESIA, 2016

"NO!" he thunders. **"We will not go!"**

The children shy away, shrink into the kitchen's corner, away from Grandpa's ire.

"We must go," his son asserts softly. "There is nothing left for us here."

"Nothing?!" Grandpa cries. "Is it nothing for a man to work his own land? Make a living with his own good hands?" He raises them, brown and gnarled; forms them into fists and shakes them in the face of his son.

He strides brusquely to the door, bangs it forcefully shut behind him. Emerges from dimness into light; a sun that beats down boldly on his aching head, his throbbing hands, his tortured heart.

He storms angrily away, across the field with its abundance of plants budding bright in the spring sun, ripe with the rain. How can they even think of going?

His fury overwhelms; irate, he forgets to turn back, to retreat before he reaches the edge, the threat he does not wish to perceive, not now, not today. But it's too late, he's seen it already, the water leaking into the farthest furrows, encroaching upon the edge of the field. His field.

Cursing he bends towards the withering plants, smells the salt and feels the loathing rise again in his heart, the hatred of his people's greatest and most ancient treasure, the source of their bounty and succor of their souls.

The wall has again failed, has let in the seawater that laps along the coast, along an ever-decreasing coast.

He turns his back on it, glares out over the remaining field, the remaining furrows filled with crops, with good fertile land but less and less of it every season, less with which to feed his family; to feed any family.

His son is waiting when he returns, gazing, like him, at the farm, half-alive, half-vanished, half-vanquished, half-gone. His grandchildren sit giggling in the dirt at its edge, patting the soil into cakes and then smashing them, sending the earth flying.

"We are going," his son repeats. "You must come, too."

Grandpa shakes his head hard, harder. "No, my son," he pronounces with conviction. "I will not go. I will not be a squatter on another man's land, earn my living by begging on doorsteps, become a scavenger, a vagabond, a homeless wanderer. A man does not abandon his native land!"

His son glances over at his children, playing cheerfully in the dirt, the soil of the country he loves, too; was born and raised to revere.

"We are not abandoning the land," he answers quietly. "It is abandoning us."

And then they are gone. Grandpa remains; watches season after season as the lapping at the shore grows nearer and louder; envelops the field and farm while he hovers at its edge, kicking the dirt, savaging the earth fast fleeing his feet.

It draws ever closer, the sea he despises. At last even his memories descend into its maw: the cakes fly no more; his grandchildren choke on a slurry of swept-away soil.

***

I had the inspiration for this story some time ago when I ran across a newspaper article about the Federated States of Micronesia, an island nation which is evidently one of the first to feel measurable and potentially disastrous effects of climate change. There is, in fact, a very real fear among the Pacific Islanders that the islands may disappear as sea level rises. Now, I have since read contrasting viewpoints – including the view that Pacific Islands that are constructed from coral reefs are in no danger from global warming because the reefs will merely grow as sea level rises, and that the disastrous predictions being made by local governments are motivated by a desire to extort financial assistance from the world's wealthier powers. However, as such arguments to me ring of the "climate change denial" that is still unfortunately so vocal and widespread, I'm not sure I'm willing to accept the science behind them without further confirmation of its accuracy.

In any case, I thought it was a concept worth exploring. Because even if the Micronesians are in no danger of losing their homelands, no one can deny that other populations have, in fact, already experienced significant, even culture-altering shifts in their native environments, particularly the Inuits of North America and other arctic peoples. Yet much as we like to believe that this problem only impacts those whose lives revolve around the ice or the sea, it affects all of us. The polar vortex that brought unusual bitter cold across the North the last two winters, the ongoing heat and drought out here in California – these are not merely matters of pleasant versus unpleasant weather. At some point they will begin to affect our ability to provide for ourselves. And how are the Canadians keeping warm when the temperature drops to forty below? By burning fuel. How are agricultural products transported to California's millions of residents? By fuel-burning trucks.

We are not merely battling climate change; climate change itself may actually increase our demands on the planet. And I, for one, am not convinced that our technology is going to be able to keep up with the pace of our environmental destruction.

My story was not overly well-received by the readers at *Every Day Fiction* – and frankly even I would agree that their criticisms of the way I've portrayed the grandfather character are justified. He is, as some pointed out, almost a caricature. And I did, in fact, think long and hard about that when I was writing the story. But in the end, this was how I saw him: as an outdated, outmoded, one-dimensional Old World character. Because to me, only such a man would continue to deny the truth of what we see transpiring around us.

MISSED CALL

Ambulance.

He stared at it, a solitary word framed in black, gray, and white; pulled from his pocket in the depths of despair. Ambulance.

It had arrived right behind him, a mere minute after he'd strolled casually up the concrete steps and into the house, cheerfully calling "Knock, knock!" as he always did, summoning her from the bedroom or office or laundry to rush out to greet him, to squeeze his chest and kiss his face as if he'd been gone a whole week and not half a day.

But not soon enough; not before he'd found her stacked in a heap on the worn kitchen floor, drenched in the sweats that meant she'd been running. Not before he'd collapsed in a heap, too, caressing her cheek and stroking her hair, wailing with the siren that was dying outside.

If only he hadn't lingered at the shop after work, cleaning his tools; if only he hadn't dawdled in the driveway to catch the end of the game on the radio. If he'd only felt the vibration in his jacket pocket over the vibration of his truck he might have hurried; been home a few minutes sooner, been by her side then instead of apprehending it now, the anguish with which she'd tried to reach him, the slew of missed calls, one following another. How she'd finally surrendered and sent him one word instead.

Ambulance.

It was only a word, a cold, meaningless word framed in black, gray, and white. Like the other words she'd sent him immediately afterwards; empty now, impossible to endure, hurtful to read. A message he could never answer, never return, never erase.

Yet he answered it anyway, beamed it hopefully, hopelessly, through the air to her body, direct to her soul.

Love you, too.

One autumn several years ago, I began having recurring and long-lasting heart palpitations. I've always been very physically active, and I was still a bit young for heart problems, but although my doctor was unable to find anything wrong with my heart, this naturally caused me a great deal of anxiety. It's difficult not to worry when your heart's pounding so hard in your chest you can see it rattling your ribcage.

This went on for some weeks without explanation. One day after I'd gone running, it hit me so badly that I quite frankly freaked out, so much so that I called my boyfriend, who, as you can probably guess, didn't answer his cell.

It's a delightful but sometimes disturbing feature of modern technology, the cell phone. Besides revolutionizing the way we communicate with one another, it has also vastly increased our expectations of being able to reach those we care about at a moment's notice. In the pre-mobile era, you never had the option of contacting a loved one from anytime or anywhere. You simply had to wait. You stared at the clock watching the minutes tick by until your child finally burst through the door yelling "Sorry I'm late!" You stared at the telephone waiting for it to ring when your husband was delayed coming home from his job. A lot of waiting, a lot of clock-staring, and a whole ton of worry.

And if the worst had, in fact, happened, there was little you could do about once you did find out. You could rush to the hospital or the scene of the accident, hoping, praying that you might be in time, that you might arrive with one minute left to spare in your loved one's life, that you might at least get the chance to say your goodbyes. But much of the time you wouldn't. It would simply be over; you'd be too late. Your child would be gone. Your husband would be dead. There would be nothing you could do but accept it.

It's different now. You hear about it every time there's a disaster, the phone calls the victims make to their friends and families, the last few moments that they are privileged to share with one another via wireless signals. And you think, how wonderful that we're now able to do that, and yet how horribly sad. How horrible it must be to receive that call, to have to listen while the most precious person in your life drowns or cries or crashes in flames to the ground. But what has to be even worse than getting that call is missing it. Knowing that you had one last chance to speak to your loved one and that you missed it because you didn't answer your phone. It's a chance you can never get back. And one that you will always regret.

Following this episode, I did some poking around online and finally discovered the cause of my heart palpitations – they were a potential side effect of the over-the-counter allergy medicine my doctor had advised me to take. I stopped using the medication and within two days my heart was behaving normally again. Who would have guessed?

I never told that boyfriend about my moment of panic or the melancholy reflections to which it had led me. But I did start trying to be more conscientious about carrying my own cell phone, just in case. I never wanted to be the one who missed the call.

THE LONG WALK HOME

She ducked; dove into them, the backwoods littered with trees, choked with leaves, infested with ferns and bracken. Sought security among them, her harshest but dearest friends; the sturdy shoots of undergrowth scraping her bare arms, tangling her feet, entwining her body with their invasive arms and fingers.

The threat was passing and she tilted; rotated her neck back towards the narrow county road, unable to resist knowing whether they had seen her; spotted her impending escape. But the unfamiliar sedan merely cruised carelessly along without stopping, even pausing; the heads of its passengers turned towards one another in deep, meaningful conversation or deep, reverent silence.

Sandra shook. She was still soaked and the early spring sun did not, perhaps could not, penetrate the dampness of the layers in which she had cloaked her back, her arms, her legs. But at least the rain had stopped, the overnight downpour that had sent her scurrying into the dark, wet wood for protection that she had failed to find; left her plodding instead through the muddy ground still sodden from the violent storms of the day or the week before, seeking in vain a flat, dry patch of dirt on which to pitch the thin canvas tent that would blunt the force of the chill wind and water.

Cautiously she emerged, peering both ways down the deserted rural highway, her ears alert for rolling intruders, invidious threats to her peace and her progress. Scraped the fresh mud off her earth-brown boots and onto the man-gray asphalt, hiked her sweat-soiled backpack higher onto her shoulders, and continued walking.

Only five miles to the next town, she reckoned, brightening as the sun struggled higher, warming her frozen face and feet while the shallow road-puddles steamed invisibly away. The thought of a real cup of coffee cheered her further, induced her almost to smile, the awkward tautening in her cheeks discomfiting her. Less than fifty miles now until it was over. Only one road more until she was free.

It was quiet here, quieter even than it had been twenty miles south or a dozen miles east, and she relished the silence, revered it; felt safe within its stillness and calm. Automobiles had grown rare, and the mechanical whine of their engines could be easily discerned now over the natural sounds of the forest: tightly packed tree-limbs whistling in the wind; fleet, furry creatures crackling through branches. Friendly noises, that covered her tread, her own whistling breaths and crackling steps. Noises surpassed only by the diligent squawking high overhead, of flocks of migrant birds flapping in formation across an increasingly azure sky, the angle formed by their flight seeming to guide her along her way; point in her direction.

She took her sandwich to go; the steaming black coffee, too, nodding politely at the cashier as if she were merely an ordinary traveler passing through: a staunch, stoic New Englander of natural reserve. Only a few days more, Sandra thought as she lifted her bag once again over her shoulders and shuffled slowly, painfully away from the town, no more than a crossroads containing a truck stop and a diner.

Perhaps she would even rest for a day before she arrived. Her pack had grown heavy and her knees sore; a small price to pay for liberty and liberation. But she didn't want to begin again on hobbled feet, swollen ankles and weary toes. Hoped to start fresh and new; momentarily, at least, free of pain.

The loveliness of afternoon was rapidly fading and she sighed, already regretting the soon-to-be-lost sunshine. Her limbs cried out for rest and she withdrew again from the road, but more purposefully, less panicky this time, setting down her pack and fishing her pocket road atlas from its depths, confirming her position, recalculating the remainder of her journey. Tucked into it, marking her place, was the flyer, the one with her face on it, a melancholy, elongated face, an ancient face, robbed of the youth it should still have possessed; an abject face, the face of misery. Numerous days and towns had passed since she'd found the paper with its pathetic, hypocritical plea; since she'd ripped it off the corner-store corkboard where it had been tacked up next to the faded announcement of the local elementary school's Easter play and a handbill hawking handymen. It was the very photograph that had prompted her to go; the one that had shocked her into realizing how unhappy she had become. The one that had boldly shown her what the timid bathroom mirror had failed to do; had exposed her life for what it really was; her future for what it really wasn't.

She folded it back into her map; packed it purposefully away. One day she might like to see it again, to compare. The face of the new woman with the face of the old.

The exhausted sun had faltered behind the pines and it was growing chill, but she was no longer weary. The sweat had ceased to drip down the crease of her spine, but the cold couldn't penetrate the warmth in her bones, the exertion of her hardening muscles. She smiled again, less clumsily this time, and it seemed to her as if the pale crescent moon that was just beginning to broach the horizon smiled back in welcome, calling her forward, leading her on, drawing her towards it like a parent teaching a child to walk. Come to Mama, come to Papa. Come.

Perhaps the line was calling, too; perhaps it always had been. She could still picture it, the back road they'd taken to bypass it with their trunk stuffed with smuggled Canadian liquor, she and her underage friends those long years before when living had still charmed and excited her; when she'd still had people with whom life could be enjoyed. What a foolish, crazy thing it had seemed at the time, ignoring the sign that commanded them to the nearest border station, whizzing gleefully, fearfully past it, southward, homeward, back to America. Young hearts clenched tight with the terror of a pursuit that didn't come; with pursuers who never came.

But now she knew it, this blind road, this charmed route that was safe from pursuers and pursuit. Had known which way to go, how not to be found, how to leave no trace upon crossing, almost as if that crazy lark had been meant to prepare her for this, the real journey, the one that counted.

She squinted in the descending darkness and wondered how long it might be, before she would dare to venture back, follow again that foolish passage through the back-roads lining the border and come home in peace, in secret. Maybe one day. When the woman she had been was long forgotten. When the woman she would be was ready to return.

The stars were winking into life and she stumbled, watching the sky and forgetting the asphalt, but she no longer cared; was no longer daunted by bruises and scrapes.

Out here there were neither homes nor streetlights to illuminate her path, only sporadic silver reflectors, working their magic only for motorists. But when she glanced into the wood she saw that it, too, was scattered with stars blinking into life, yellow and brown ones that reflected and stared but didn't menace, didn't unnerve her. Glowed instead like a hundred tiny flashlights lighting her way; dozens of mysterious, mystical guides; strange, silent, but loyal friends, like the moon overhead and the stars up above, anonymous benefactors who had at last taken an interest in helping, protecting, caring for her.

She closed her eyes against the darkness and it fell away; cloaked her as she clunked soft and straight along the side of the silent highway, treading the invisible white line with heavy, hurting feet and picturing the bridge, the passage into hope, away from desperation. Imagined it instead as a falls, a powerful shower that would purge and restore, wash away her frustration and fear, grant her renewal and rebirth: a baptism by border crossing. A welcoming wall of water on the other side of which she would emerge, clean and bright and unknown to anyone; unknown to all.

Just a little further tonight, she thought, urging her tender feet to follow faster after the twinkling lights in the forest, to overtake the moon and stars. Just a little bit more, and I'll be there that much sooner.

Her heart ached. She kept walking.

WAITING

The following long short story was originally inspired by the History Channel program *Life After People.* The premise of the show is not to examine the potential causes of the end of humanity, but rather "what happens to the world we leave behind."

It's a fascinating program. It details the fates of our roads, our cities, our buildings, even our family pets and other creatures who depend upon us for a living. It quite often comes to the rather disturbing conclusion that in a pretty short space of planetary time – mere hundreds of years, not thousands – we will be completely forgotten by an Earth that may fare better without us.

"Waiting" tells the story of a middle-aged misanthrope who witnesses this degeneration, who lives long enough to see how quickly humanity can fail, how insufficient its infrastructure is in the case of a massive disaster. But what place is there for a person in a world without people?

Often I think about all of the species that ours is driving into extinction, and I wonder how those creatures must feel as their communal days draw to an end – varieties of birds chirping and dancing, trying to attract mates who no can longer hear or see them, tigers prowling through jungles, finding plenty of food for their young but no young with whom to share it, whales sending their songs out into empty oceans, wondering why none of their kind will sing them an answer. Would our end be any different? With nothing but the power of our own feet and voices to seek out other humans, how would we even find those who had survived a disaster or epidemic? How would it feel to be so completely alone?

Our society has produced enough in the way of non-perishable commodities where small groups of people could probably survive for a very long time purely on the remnants of our lost civilization. And I have to wonder, if the survivors were sufficiently few, would they even try to do more than live out the years that remained them? Would a couple or a half-dozen survivors attempt to rebuild, to resume agriculture, to begin repopulating a planet with a handful of children, many of whom would once again die in utero or in early infancy? Or would they merely spend their time waiting, waiting for their own time to be over and for peace at last to come to the planet?

Under what circumstances would we be prepared to simply surrender and say our goodbyes?

It's the Summer of '19 and I'm sitting here in the heart of America waiting for the world to end. That's silly, some might say, because for all practical purposes, from the point of view of humanity, anyway, the world already has ended; but for me it hasn't yet and that's why I'm still waiting.

It might seem even sillier for me to be writing about awaiting the end of the world when it is readily apparent that no one is ever going to read my account, however intriguing and fascinating it may be, nor refer to it as an historical document, no matter how informative and accurate it is. I know it's silly, probably ludicrously so, but I figure there is a chance, however slight, that somewhere in the world, perhaps even in the unexplored depths of these formerly united former states, someone may yet linger who reads and comprehends English; perhaps someone who will emerge a decade hence from a secret underground civilization built within a protected bubble, some scientific or militaristic experiment formulating a contingency plan for American citizens in case of deadly asteroid or nuclear missile attack, someone who will one day rise to a lonely surface and wonder, "What the fuck??!!" Or, perhaps, if it turns out that those who believe that technology was given to ancient civilizations by advanced aliens wishing humanity to thrive and prosper have been right all along, then maybe in a few thousand years when the aliens decide to re-visit our planet they'll find it reassuring to learn that no, we did not, in fact, blow ourselves up in consequence of the knowledge they so recklessly imparted into our adolescent, immature hands, as seemed likely for so long, but were destroyed by natural causes like every other extinct species on the planet. Except, of course, for those which were destroyed by man.

It started in California, not far from where I lived halfway up the coast by the Bay. It's not all that surprising that that's where it started, because California was a mecca for both immigrants and tourists from other states and countries, and its coastline was thickly and perpetually packed with people: people crowded into condos and townhomes and tiny studio apartments and single-family houses stacked tight on top of other single-family houses. It was the weather, they said; and although it was hard to imagine that weather could stand up by itself against exorbitantly priced property, top-ranking taxes, horrendously heavy traffic, and a resilient routine of catastrophic earthquakes, mudslides, and wildfires, I continued to live there, too, so there must have been something in it at that.

But whether it was the weather or no, California was packed with people, San Francisco nearly as much as Los Angeles; people flying and driving and bike-riding in and out of town every day and carrying it with them wherever they went, so even if California wasn't where it originated, it was certainly where it took hold and spread. And when you've got that many people podded together into one comparatively small area, things like that disseminate quickly, and also the cases grow rapidly more noticeable because they're so close together, and pretty soon it looks like you've got an epidemic even when you don't.

And maybe that's why, in spite of the dire reports that started filtering over the airwaves to my car radio, that I didn't think about it that much at first. The media always exaggerates, right? Everything signifies impending doom. When someone at my office caught it, I didn't think much of it either, nor when the dude in the cubicle next to hers came down with it, too, for the simple reason that I'd always suspected they were secretly getting it on in the janitor's closet at lunchtime because once I saw him coming out of there wearing a shit-eating grin and a few minutes later I ran into her at the copy machine and her breath smelled like semen. Besides, that's how it is when you work in an office: everyone catches everything everyone else has, as well as everything their kids bring home from school or from the germ-infested houses of their snotty-nosed friends. But then that lady and the guy I thought she was humping didn't come back to work and I heard rumors they were in the hospital, and then the queer quiet little fellow who sat slack-jawed across from me began hacking up a storm through his open and suddenly much louder mouth, and then his neighbor got it, too, and the woman next to him, and without warning my phone was ringing off the hook because apart from me, practically my whole department was out sick all at once. Except for my boss, whom I wouldn't have minded seeing hacking up a lung onto the graying carpet that he never had cleaned, and over which my rolling chair obstinately refused to roll, it was so sticky. Then the janitor caught it, too, which would have freed up his closet for round-the-clock side-door shenanigans except that the lady and her lover had died and we closed up the office for an afternoon to attend their funerals, me in the stiff black high-collared dress I'd bought twenty years before for just such rare occasions, and which I heartily hated nearly as much as the ridiculous strappy pumps that went with it.

I didn't have to suffer through hours and days of somber ceremony, affected solemnity, and enforced sobriety for long, though. Because pretty soon after, my other cubicle-mates had died, too, and so had the janitor, and now my neighbors at the apartment building were catching it, and funerals were suddenly being pushed back, way back, three or four weeks even, because the short-term demand had become greater than the immediate supply, and there simply wasn't enough time to get everyone buried both properly and promptly. In a flash morticians became as highly sought after as manicurists and embalming rates skyrocketed, leaving one to wonder whether the caretakers of our future corpses were truly as ethical as one might theretofore have liked to believe.

But I don't think I actually started to worry until my boss fell sick, my wretched asshole of a boss who invariably infuriated me with his foul breath on my neck while I was trying to talk our idiot clients through troubleshooting the functioning of their small kitchen appliances, a distraction from my duties that I needed about as much as his stilted-speech lectures on what was wrong with my tone in delivering the rote phrases I reiterated day in and out, most common of which was "Is it plugged in?" I knew it was serious when he abruptly disconnected me from the six calls I had on hold with customers from across the country and beckoned me into his office with that familiar obnoxious crook of his finger and a rare half a smile perking up his drooping chin.

"Sharon," he whispered, licking his lips. Not in a gross, leering way, mind; more like they were chapped and he was trying to moisten them. They certainly looked dried out, cracked and a bit bloody, which was no wonder after all that coughing and labored respiration. "Go on home, Sharon."

"Excuse me?" I replied, forgetting to add the "sir," a cardinal sin around our workplace. Of course, he'd just called me by my first name, so I figured he had no right to complain about my sudden lack of strict professional propriety.

He didn't even seem to notice it. "Go home," he urged. "Be with your loved ones."

I had no loved ones to speak of and, oddly enough, my curiosity was more powerful than my desire to depart my dreaded cubicle so unprecedentedly before noon, which prompted me to pose a very natural if, in retrospect, arguably asinine question. "How come?"

He swallowed and choked back a cough with effort. "We're done here, Sharon. Haven't you noticed that everyone else is gone?"

Well, sure, of course I had. I never had to wait for the elevator or the toilet anymore, but since that was sure to be temporary, I had decided to enjoy it while it lasted without concerning myself too greatly as to the cause.

"They'll be back, though, won't they, sir?" I inquired, remembering my manners this time.

He didn't answer, but gently, almost humanely wobbled his close-shorn head with its assortment of ragged bumps poking up through the fine frosted hair. "I doubt it, Sharon. Most likely I won't be back either, after today." He sighed with such melancholy that I was almost moved. "I've prepared your final check. I had to hand-write it – the payroll department's been out for a while now and I can't figure out how to work that stupid program – but the bank can call me if they have any questions."

I accepted the blotted slip of paper from his shaking hands while he examined me with moist, lethargic eyes. There was a month's severance pay included. I was so astonished that I'll be damned if I didn't begin to protest and re-evaluate whether I'd been entirely fair in my opinion of Mr. Boss-man.

"Take the money, Sharon," he insisted. "Enjoy it; it may not be good to you much longer." He fell back in his chair, politely declining to shake my hand as I thanked him, and disintegrating visibly into relief as I turned to walk away.

It took me the short ride down the elevator and long hike out to the parking lot to comprehend his comment about the check. "It may not be good to you much longer." Checks didn't go stale for a year, did they? Then I got it. The company was shutting down, right? He must have meant the check might bounce, or that he was closing the account soon or something like that. Well, I was no fool; if I was going to be out of work a while I would need that money, so I took the check right to the bank and cashed it in for a fat pile of crisp new hundred-dollar bills, walking away from the teller with a heap so tall and clean I must have looked like I was stuffing Christmas cards for all three dozen of my nonexistent grandchildren.

So although I'd rather abruptly found myself

unemployed, I was not altogether unhappy when I arrived back at the unusually spacious one-bedroom apartment that half of my weekly pay went to maintain. There were a lot of sick people in my neighborhood, too – I knew it not merely by the noise of their hacking seeping through their faceless walls and vacant yards, but by the lack of traffic on our avenue, which was no minor thoroughfare and directly positioned en route to the freeway – but I'd always been such a firm believer in respecting the privacy of one's neighbors that I'd never really gotten to know the fellow-residents of my street, and thus was not particularly observant of nor alarmed by perils to their well-being so long as they were not imposed upon me.

On this particular day, however, an even worse threat than unexplained incurable illness had struck home, for blasting into my apartment came the non-stop screeching of the infant brat of the single woman who inhabited the unit below mine, a startlingly strong successor in volume to the mere retching from the woman herself that had interrupted my restful slumber the previous evening and compelled me to arrive at the office in an even worse temper than was usual for a Tuesday morning. At length I called the super but couldn't reach him; left a message requesting he go warn my neighbor to shut up her damned kid or get out. Whether he ever responded or not I couldn't tell, but some hours later the whiny brat finally ceased its infernal racket as if at last worn out or sick of crying. After dinner I dozed fitfully, and was awoken in full again in the wee hours of the morning by renewed screaming from the aforementioned loudmouth, bawling which pierced my subconscious like a jackhammer, sending me lunging for the medicine cabinet and making me wish I was a morning drinker.

It must be teething, I seethed silently to myself,

recollecting that this was painful for infants and futilely seeking the compassion that ought to have filled my heart upon recognition of the poor undeserving creature's unavoidable ailment. Although failing to find the requisite sympathy within, I did recover some measure of my good humor after drowning my vexation in a fresh batch of homebrew, the super-strong concoction that I called coffee and that everyone else referred to as boiled tar. Recollecting, also, that I did not have to go to work that day and face the phone with the moronic callers chirping on about their malfunctioning or paranormally possessed appliances and the boss who refused ever to let me call them idiots even when they really, really deserved it, I was nearly cheerful as I emerged with my thermos into the fine wispy fog and made my way downtown in a rare pre-dawn walk to the marina.

I loved the marina as I loved few places on earth, and far more than I cared for most of humanity; especially at late night or early morning, when it was entirely devoid of those people with their provoking mad chatter that ruined the serenity of the bay and the boats, and on this particular morning it bore an air of exceptionally eerie calm and quiet, and even I hushed my footsteps as I trod softly along the wood-slatted pier, gazing in awe at the magnificent boats I did not know how to sail or drive or whatever you called what you did with them. The late moon was carved into irregular halves of black and white and still shone down upon the shore, glinting off the metal railings and silver poles, while the salty water lapped tranquilly against the posts of the pier as if it had never been subjected to a harsh wind or word.

All at once the peacefulness of the scene was broken when, in the periphery of my vision, I espied a fluttering in a somewhat larger-than-average craft some dozen yards ahead of me, a flapping that sounded more animal than human and that consequently inspired in me more curiosity than apprehension, although, it being a dark and rather creepy almost-morning, I was not entirely free of the latter sensation. But I continued my stroll, cautiously muting my breath and step, peeling my eyes in the vain hope of expanding my pupils in the waning moonlight, and even refraining from slurping the now rapidly cooling coffee from my thermos in my desire to preserve the secrecy of my presence. As I drew nearer, the noise of fluttering increased, and a slight squawking was added to it, and even before the suspicion had firmly formed in my mind, they had materialized before me, a festering flock of seagulls gathered about the deck of a small yacht, tearing with their yellow beaks at the corpse of what could only have been a man lying prone and quite dead on the deck.

It was in that moment that I grew scared. I had never voluntarily abandoned the marina mid-stroll but I did so now, attempting and failing to reassure myself that the man on the yacht had merely been murdered, probably for diddling some drug-dealer's dame, and that there was absolutely no reason to believe that I might share the same fate. I hurried back to my apartment, so intent on my purpose I even forgot to finish the remainder of the swill swishing against the lid of my cup, and finally determined to find out just how serious this thing was. But as if my eyes had at last been opened to the condition of the swelter of humanity that had heretofore constantly crowded me, the answer to my unspoken question became increasingly apparent as I drew near to home. Morning was breaking, but still no one besides me was out on the street, not even the pre-dawn dog- and baby-walkers that usually irked me with their whining, pooping pooches and whining, pooping children. And since when had that greasy cholesterol factory they called a donut shop been closed during prime breakfast hours? When was the normally trash-ridden parking lot of the twenty-four-hour supermarket ever empty of cars as well as of garbage? Even the stink of the piss on the sidewalk near the clandestine homeless encampment beneath the overpass seemed to be fading, and, for that matter, I couldn't recall the last time my spare change had been politely requested by either a man or a woman desperately in need of a shave.

I hurried faster; burst in, even, to my warm welcoming kitchen with its hot remnants of cooked coffee and suggestive promise of bacon and eggs for breakfast and turned on the television, loudly enough to cover the noise of the baby who was still wailing below, if with considerably less energy.

She looked terrible. I'd always despised this particular anchorwoman for being both charming and beautiful in a way I never had been, and at my age now never would be, but even so, today I thought I stood a solid chance of outperforming her at a beauty pageant or talent competition unless it was for the walking undead, who presumably operate under different standards than those of us who are alive and like it that way. She was difficult to comprehend, being racked with a fit of coughing every few sentences, while the cue cards were changed audibly by a man who coughed equally audibly from behind the camera. She was throwing around fancy medical terms like "plague" and "pandemic" and less scientific ones like "terror" and "panic" and the physician she purported to interview by satellite was wearing a face mask and stuttering himself in spite of it. His calm reassurances might have been more comforting had they not centered entirely around vague mystical concepts such as "international cooperation" and "Third-World vaccination" and "universal healthcare," and the uniformed official who followed him offering unconvincing evidence that the federal government had the situation firmly under control only served to persuade me that the country must have fallen into some truly unprecedented pile of deep shit.

Very definitely afraid now, I vaulted the stairs down to my car and high-tailed it to the grocery store, struggling to recollect snatches of reality shows focusing on abnormal behaviors like hoarding and preparing for apocalypse, and wishing that I had paused longer on what I now understood were invaluable educational programs before changing over to the travel and cartoon channels. I pushed the cart through the nearly vacant aisles, loading up on cold cereal and granola bars, canned foods and bottled water, toilet paper and ground coffee, the things I thought you were supposed to stock up on when you were facing a natural catastrophe. A few others were cruising the supermarket with me. A harassed-looking mother with a listless middle-school aged child perusing the pharmaceuticals; a teenager with the pockets of his bulky jacket bulging lingering in the liquor aisle; an elderly man in the produce section half-heartedly squeezing the kiwis and mangos in turn, trying to select the choicest fruit from among the softening carcasses; stock that hadn't been turned over lately. And at the cash register stood a pimply-faced youth with sandy hair and a pale, clammy complexion.

"That will be, um, eighty dollars," he said, glancing over the vast heap of contents overflowing the cart I was straining to push.

"Aren't you going to ring it up?" I inquired, raising my eyebrows sternly at the awkward young man, certain that my total should be at least twice what he was asking.

He colored; glanced hopelessly about. "The manager

went home sick," he explained. "I'm just a bag boy; I don't know how to work the register," he confessed.

I handed over my credit card but he shook his head; didn't know how to operate that machine either. I yanked out one of my fresh clean hundreds. "Keep the change," I insisted as he struggled with a fat envelope stacked sloppily with bills, pitying and nearly admiring the work ethic of the youth who stood steadfast in his position when his slack co-workers had retreated and fled. As I wheeled my mountain of goods towards the exit I turned and saw him carefully tucking my hundred dollars into the envelope; withdrawing twenty from it and then marking the total, wiping his nose with his sleeve as he did so, and was shocked to realize that he might be dead soon and even more shocked to realize that I'd feel a bit sorry for the poor kid if he was.

The neighbor's baby had finally stopped crying. The silence struck me more ominously than the noise had, prompting me even to call the super again and leave a message of less ire and greater concern. Still I stayed out of it; didn't go to investigate, figuring my neighbor's business was none of my affair any more than mine was hers. In fact, for the next two days I kept my nose out of everyone's business; stayed in my apartment with the blinds nearly closed, tilted open just barely enough to let in the sun that strayed weakly into my living room as if it didn't want to be there any more than I did. But as I saw no point in going outdoors, I spent my hours catching up on my reading and correspondence, applying for unemployment and searching the job listings, of which there had been a slew several weeks prior and hardly any in the last few days.

On the third day the morning dawned cold, and I was snatched from my sleep-stupor by a sickly-sweet aroma creeping out through the heater-vent in my bedroom wall.

It wasn't unusual for the heater ducts to smell funny on their first usage in the late fall, and at first I thought nothing of it, except that the odor seemed strange, more repugnant than usual. When it persisted into the afternoon I began to feel nauseated, and went down to the super's apartment to see if I might surprise him at home since he obviously had no intention of ever returning my calls.

I knocked. There was no answer. I knocked harder. Still no answer. By then I'd been cooped up with that nasty stench in my apartment all day and the smell, if anything, was even more cloying out here in the hall and I was fed up; I'd had it with the stinking super and his stinking building and I battered his door with my fists loudly enough to draw a horde of outraged tenants into the open, although for some mysterious reason no one else appeared. And then my fists hurt and that made me angrier, so I jiggled the doorknob in my frustration and didn't bother to attempt to conceal my astonishment when the door opened.

I shouldn't have gone inside. I should have known better, but I didn't. The super was there, of course. He and his wife and five children, all clustered together as if they had merely lain down for a nap on the hardwood floor of their living room and overslept by a matter of several long days. As if the floor had been their last refuge from the disaster overtaking them and they'd poised themselves upon it in tight linear array to await the end, hoping, perhaps, that by lining themselves up in such neat order that the mortician might attend to them first; bypass the families who'd had the gall to drop dead in an untidy tangle.

I might have stood it had it not been for the flies. But somehow seeing them buzzing about the open mouths of the family's faces was a hundred times worse than the hollow faces themselves, and I slammed the door shut quickly behind me and pummeled the neighbor's door instead.

"It's Sharon!" I shouted. "From 3B!" But no one answered, not at that door and not at the next one either and then I did it, I went up to 2B and pounded nearly hard enough to wake the dead or, at the very least, a teething infant if there was still one in there.

There was no answer there either. I attempted my trick of jiggling the doorknob but nothing happened, and I knew, I knew that although no one would stop me if I tried it, that I could not return to the super's place to retrieve his keys and so instead I went up to my own apartment and cautiously climbed down the fire escape to the second floor balcony and found, to my grim pleasure and eternal chagrin, that the slider was open.

At least I wasn't caught off guard this time. She was long gone, the neighbor lady, and her kid was so quiet I thought he must be, too. But when I prodded his tiny form in the crib in which he lay so fusslessly napping, he gurgled a bit, and I reluctantly removed him from his wood-slatted cage. He stunk of piss and shit but it still seemed way more natural than the way she stunk, so I hauled him over to the sink and rinsed his bottom with the faucet until it passed for sanitary – the bottom, not the sink – and then fumbled my way through contorting him into a new diaper that I extracted from a box on the floor. I checked the cupboard and found formula and a bottle, so I loaded up the baby bag the unfortunate mother had so thoughtfully left packed for us, and trudged with my goods and child through the apartment to the front door and went back upstairs to my own place to feed him.

He took it greedily, sucking hard with that horrible disgusting slurping noise that babies make when they're at their mother's tits, so I switched on the television again to try to drown out the noise. I was aided in this endeavor by the blaring beeps of the emergency broadcast system, which played over and over until I loathed it more than the suckling noises and turned off the TV and listened to the kid chomping the rubber nipple instead.

As he finally fell back into a restless sleep in the suitcase full of towels I'd laid out for him, I wondered what the hell I was going to do with this wee but troublesome nuisance. His mother was obviously gone, and if he had a father, I'd never seen him. Did he have any other relations who could take him in? Should I call Social Services?

I was reluctant to do either, and by this time I wasn't fooling myself anymore; I knew damned well why. No one was going to answer the phone at Social Services because if the TV wasn't even working, they sure as hell wouldn't be either, and even if I could find out who they were, any relations the poor kid might have had were likely sick or dead, too. Me, I'd never wanted a kid any more than I'd wanted a man to look after, and the thought of dragging some sniveling snot around with me, feeding it and disposing of its excrement until this whole situation resolved itself, was almost more than I could bear. But even more unbearable was the thought of sticking it back in that reeking apartment with its dead mother and the insects that were already harassing her and leaving it there to die like a spider caught in a bathtub when the water starts running. No, that I could not do. I might not want the kid but I wouldn't put it through that, either. I wouldn't put a feral dog through that, even if it bit me.

I resigned myself to it as I began tossing my things into my other suitcases, the ones not occupied by the snoozing infant whose name I didn't know and didn't care to discover. I couldn't stay any longer. The stench was growing intolerable and I was grateful that it was November; imagined how much worse it would be if it were warm. On the other hand it was November, and if the heater stopped working that was going to get really unpleasant very quickly, particularly if I was stuck indoors with a bunch of corpses and carrion-feeders.

I checked on the kid. The intrepid little squirt coughed up a bit and slept on, as oblivious to my grownup problems as I was to his infant ones. I understood it now, his ceaseless wailing. His mother had probably dropped dead those three days ago; left him alone and hungry with nothing to do but cry for help into an unseeing, unhearing, nearly unoccupied void. A cry that no one answered.

Well, how the hell was I supposed to know? I thought irritably. Babies cry. Sometimes they don't shut up. How could I have known its mother was dead? And anyway, was that even my problem?

It was now, I thought grimly as I stepped into the last hot shower I might enjoy for a while. I was stuck with that kid but good, and I figured I'd better hit the store again and stock up on formula before I left town. Although it wasn't crying, it sounded thirsty again already; was coughing dryly as if its throat ached, and its skin was pale and clammy as if it was seriously dehydrated, which was only to be expected under the circumstances. I warmed up another bottle on the stove and offered it to him but he wouldn't take it; merely turned his head and coughed harder, louder, and then I went pale and clammy myself and backed away from the open suitcase and retreated into the bedroom and packed faster, ignoring the noise in the kitchen and at the same time waiting for it to stop.

By the end of the day I had the car loaded with an array of clothes and hygiene products as well as an enormous new stash of non-perishables raided from the supermarket down the street, now entirely unmanned and with a giant hole smashed through its glass front window. The harassed-looking mother still lingered among the pharmaceuticals but her kid was nowhere to be seen; had presumably outlived her. The looters hadn't done a very good job of it, either. Even the alcohol aisle had barely been touched and I thought of the teen; wondered if he'd enjoyed his first and probably last taste of liquor.

I'd left the kid home while I shopped, my door recklessly unlocked. He'd been alone for days already, I thought, so what was the harm? Besides, I couldn't postpone going out; I wanted to be ready as soon as it was time. I checked on him when I got back. It wasn't time yet.

In the morning the time had finally come, and I wrapped the now still and silent little bugger in one of the soft clean towels from the suitcase and tiptoed back down the fire escape and slipped him in through the slider before creeping quietly away, as if I were afraid of waking him. He at least ought to be found with his mother, I thought crossly, when someone finally came to sort them out. If anyone ever came to sort them out.

And then I took off, screeched my way fast out of the apartment parking-lot and then crawled slowly through the streets of town, navigating the roads devoid of cars but littered with bodies; scaring away the crows and coyotes that were already emerging from the hills and daring to invade the city streets, lured by the smell of fresh flesh and blood. Found the freeway abandoned except for pile-ups scattered in random pockets across the lanes; their drivers hours or days past resuscitation. Others had apparently tried to make a break for it long before I had; had been quicker on the uptake, but failures nonetheless. Just as well, I thought, chills tingling my spine. Those who had succeeded had probably taken it with them, carried it up and down the coast, infecting even the small, the insignificant towns where everyone stopped but neglected to stay. Brought it in and then left it behind them.

South of Gilroy the cities vanished and the roads cleared. The air cleared, too; the aroma of garlic overpowering the odor of death. But I didn't stop, seek succor there; no, I wasn't fooled by that, not this time, not ever again.

By San Luis Obispo I needed gas. I held my breath in taut expectation and expelled it in relieved gratitude when the pump worked, automated beyond human need or control. I wondered how long that would last.

At Ventura the fog astonished me by breaking mid-day; reminding me that L.A. was ahead and that I didn't want to go there, so I detoured across the mountains instead, thankfully still free of snow, but blanketed nonetheless by a dense, putrid layer of smog, smog that smelled different from the usual combustion-engine pallor, but which hung no less thickly in the air around. I shut my windows, opened a box of cereal and munched it plain; gorged myself on pears and tangerines, the last fresh fruit I might see for some time. And kept driving, never stopped driving, and when I finally pulled over at a rest area hours past my usual bedtime, I was across the border and spending my first night on the road in Arizona.

In the morning I woke to a bright, fresh new world. The air was pure and clean-smelling and I sucked it in, savored it, stretched my cramped legs and feet in the cool crispness of desert dawn, fingered my neat stack of new hundred-dollar bills, and considered my options.

I was out, out of California. Surely here I would be rid of it, rid of the foul stench of urban life and its increasing decay. But no, it had beaten me there, too. There were no cars going by on the highway, but there were other cars surrounding me in the rest stop, cars whose drivers slept heavily, unmoving in the rising dawn, cars with California plates with drivers who had tried, just like me, to escape; had come this far and then gone no further.

I resumed my drive. I switched on the radio again but there was no signal way out there; probably wouldn't have been anyway. When I finally located a station on the outskirts of Flagstaff, a hushed voice spoke to me in Mexican-Spanish, intoning a prayer in a foreign tongue that I didn't comprehend, and quickly lapsing into ceaseless silence.

I avoided the town. It wasn't large, but I knew what I'd find there and didn't need to see it. I shopped for supplies a ways up the road; plundered another unmanned grocery for water and food and didn't bother to leave my money on the counter; didn't bother to check the hut behind the shop for the absent owner, not there, nor at the truck-stop fuel pump that cheerfully accepted my credit card, not knowing that things like credit and cash hardly mattered anymore.

Cities set me to cringing; the country called. I'd never been out-of-state before and I pretended my journey was part of a plan, a gloriously prolonged holiday intended for sightseeing. Arizona was gorgeous, magnificent; it seemed natural void, empty except for the cacti and coyotes and common carrion creatures. Its features beckoned, dazzled me into forgetfulness: the Painted Desert with its color-streaked strata; the Petrified Forest with its hewn trees of stone. Vast Meteor Crater, a mere pockmark on the Earth's surface when viewed from the heavens but a deep, sandy valley from the railing around, memory of an age-old disaster from eons before. So much more awe-inspiring than my first stop had been, at the edge of the cavernous Canyon, the view from its rim ruined by the mass of visitors choked up on its ropes. Visitors who might have brought it in with them, or taken it home; international tourists boarding the next bus, the next train, the next flight to anywhere, everywhere.

In New Mexico I dawdled; drifted through Gallup, its wide empty streets maintained with care by residents who revered the dead and scavengers who didn't. I grew bold in the vacuum, raiding the supermarket refrigerators that had been so thoughtfully left running, consuming the electricity already generated by wind and water and maintained for a time by machines; power for which no one would ever pay. Ducked past Albuquerque with my windows rolled tight and didn't catch my breath until Carlsbad, its creepy caverns still eerily lit with solar-powered bulbs; its bats even more screechy and numerous than I'd heard or imagined.

Texas was worst; brought it wholly home. I couldn't not stop, I'd always wanted to see it; but the Alamo was littered with them, furry four-legged animals running with bones; vultures picking at their leftover leavings. The river ran by it but I couldn't stomach a swim; kept my eyes on the ornamental buildings and shunned the view of the clogged waterway still struggling through town.

Along the Gulf I found relief: like the desert, its shores seemed natural forsaken by all but the wild. I'd been avoiding human haunts, the places where people might have lived or died, but in the heart of Louisiana I couldn't resist; I gazed with amazement at the houses on stilts lining its coast; was overcome by the urge to see inside of one, to climb the stairs and watch the water filling the nonexistent floor beneath.

I chose a well-kept, pretty blue one attended by an ancient sedan, dusty like they were all rapidly becoming in between rains. I rang the bell, even knocked out of habit, but didn't hesitate when I got no answer; twirled the doorknob and went inside as if I owned the place, which, I supposed, I did, if concepts like real estate any longer had value or meaning.

Apart from its unique structure, it was a house like any other, but I was charmed nonetheless, by the cheerful gold curtains draping its windows, the grandchildren-photographs lining its mantle, the quaint puffy sofas furnishing its parlor; some strange remnant of happy-go-lucky humanity in all its foolhardy glory. I even wondered if perhaps I should settle there for a time; make myself at home and relax on the bayou while awaiting its passing. And then I heard a noise overhead and my sense of proprietorship was offended; resolutely I ascended the hard wooden stairs, brashly determined to chuck out the family of possums or alligators that had unscrupulously invaded my intended new domicile.

She was past aid; that was evident from the odor and the clinging of the thin sheet to her sunken form, which outlined the hollows that had become more pronounced since her death some days before. But he still lingered, staring blankly at her and piteously at me, the blithe bold intruder; haggard and inhuman but conscious, aware.

"Stay back," he warned. "You don't want to get sick."

I crouched in the doorway, diverting my eyes from the shroud so nearby.

"I guess we caught it," he mumbled. "I called for help but no one came."

I didn't answer. There was no point in telling him that no help existed.

From several feet away he reached out towards me and I feared, knew the absurdity of fearing but felt it nonetheless; the instinct intruding. Swallowed and quenched it while he sought to stretch out with his hand but failed to engage it; settled for a twitch of his fingers instead.

"She was a God-fearing woman," he choked. "She wouldn't have liked it; no decent burial."

A cough rasped in his throat but he struggled on; forced the words out. "Her folks are buried right here in town. After… after, young lady, if you could…we bought our plots already…"

I nodded. Not in agreement, but in my haste to silence him, shut out the image, the knowledge of what he was asking. He closed his eyes and lay silently, patiently, and I grew angry with his calm stoicism, the burden that he was forcing upon me in consequence of it.

"It doesn't matter anymore!" I wanted to shout. What were two insignificant corpses anyway, and why should I care where they were laid to rest, or if they rested at all? But he staved off my protest; let out a gasp and then breathed no more, almost as if he had only been waiting for some savior to arrive, a savior not of life but of death, who would reassure him of consecration; give him peace in ignorance, and ignorance in peace. A pointless, pathetic, pitiful peace.

But I did it. Scowling and grumbling, I did it. Just like the baby in the apartment below; I couldn't help myself; couldn't refuse the dying man's last wish, however crazy and futile it seemed to me now. Grudgingly I ransacked the house until I unearthed the marriage license divulging her maiden name, then traipsed through the cemetery in the heart of town until I found it, the family plot that would have plenty of room now, room for many more than would ever find rest there. Wrapped their decimated figures disgustedly in big blankets from the linen closet and dragged them down the stairs to their own aged sedan; stole a pickaxe and a shovel from the keeper's shed and achingly dug out a shallow grave deep and wide enough for two consorts in life, companions in death. When it was finished, I abandoned their car and walked back to the house, to my own vehicle that waited tranquil and free, free yet of the stench of death and decay, free yet of the burdens of the dead and the dying.

After that I didn't go into any more houses. I didn't want to take a chance on finding more dying, which was far worse than finding more dead. I didn't think I could stand having any more promises to keep; more senseless, fruitless pledges to the doomed, the ended, the over.

I took again to the perimeter, not quite knowing why; skirted the edge of the country as I'd skirted the cities, tarrying in parks and along the shoreline; spending, expanding what was left of my time. In Mobile the gas or the mechanisms that worked it finally failed. I tried every pump at the station I'd stopped at, and the one across the street and down the block as well, but couldn't suck up a drop and had to steal it from an ownerless SUV, wielding a siphon I'd had the foresight to snatch from an auto-parts store that I'd raided for oil.

I needed the fuel. In Florida the lights died altogether, prompting me to flee the frightful pitch-blackness of the steamy wild Everglades; take up the coast to the white Carolina beaches. By early spring I had invaded the capital, admiring the majestic and now meaningless monuments to powerful presidents, pursuers of happiness, promoters of peace. Plundered the museums and found odd amusements within; perched on the Wright Brothers' plane and fought the Red Baron, taking vengeance for the bodies that lay strewn in the hall.

I took the long way around, exploring Dutch country now barren of Amish; bypassing the rot, the rats of New York, the subways that might even now be filling with sea; travelling instead up through small-town New England with its thick grassy lawns and thick-wooded yards; along the cold coast of Maine with its hardy fauna and flora, moose and white pines.

And then I turned back, turned inland, still seeking a smoke, a fire, some sign of survival, but finding nothing, none, hardly ever even whole dead ones anymore; scattered parts, pieces of people I'd never been interested in knowing and now never would know. And wondered, why me? Why wasn't I sick? Maybe I hadn't liked them much, people with their annoying habits, unreasoning expectations, and indelicate demands. Yet they had been mine, my people nonetheless, and it might be a very long lifetime if I had to spend it being irked and irritated by the cats and coyotes instead of my own kind. How would I live, a stranger in my own country, on my own planet? What was I supposed to do with myself now, if they were all gone? Who was I without them? What was the point of me, myself, alone? It didn't seem right, or fair, somehow, that only I should survive. Shouldn't I, too, go the way of the rest? Did they deserve to die any more, or me any less?

But I made the most of it, my new life without people. I went everywhere; through all of the landscapes I'd ever wanted to see and even those I didn't; every place in the country in which humans were the least noteworthy of attractions. Through the dense fogs of West Virginia and the wispy mists of the Smoky Mountains; the flats of Nebraska, the prairies of Kansas, the hills of Colorado. Utah with its fantastic rock formations; bridges and arches in red, yellow, and gold; dinosaur skeletons carved into stone. At last gave up on finding; wasn't even sure anymore if I wanted to find. Acquiesced to aloneness, to rareness, impending extinction. Maybe not actually the last of the species but one of the few and far-between. Like the endangered creature who refuses to mate, who knows that reproduction is futile; the end is too near.

And finally the last leg had gone. I'd driven the

Loneliest Road and crunched across the moonscape of Idaho; seen what was left of the glaciers and stood under the Tetons. And now I stand here, at the end of my road, awaiting the end. Waiting with hope.

I've placed my bet and it's on Yellowstone, iconic symbol of these formerly united former states, former home to former Americans, former objective of former explorers; future destructor of the life which remains. It's laid out before me; its boiling pots steaming cheerfully while a herd of buffalo both big and small graze its greenery short and crisp, ignoring the wolf-pack howling in the invisible distance; the lone weaponless human no longer posing a threat to either predator or prey.

They predicted it decades ago, the long-overdue volcanic eruption that might doom the species. Posited year-round winters of cruel dust and bitter ash that would shut out the sun and starve away life. The joke's on them, now. The crater's been beaten; outpaced by the tiniest of competitors, the smallest of viruses with the deadliest of impacts. One lone woman is all that's left for it now: a fluke survivor, an unnaturally immune, unwitting witness to the end of it all.

It smells here, too, but not of sickness and death. Of promise. I watched the world end once; why not again? And for good this time. Because where I sit there's no doubt that if it happens, it will take me with it. Take me to the place where all the rest of the people are, everywhere and nowhere all at once. To where I belong now.

I'm ready for it: the celebration, the final show. Got a fresh clean stack of crisp hundred-dollar bills, mint-condition confetti with which to hail the beginning and end. To tear up and let flutter down like so much dust and ash over fields of green, fields of grain, fields of flame.

And anyway I have nothing left to do now but wait.

ABOUT THE AUTHOR

Lori Schafer is a writer of serious prose and humorous erotica and romance. Her flash fiction, short stories, and essays have appeared in numerous print and online publications, and her first two books were published in November 2014. *On Hearing of My Mother's Death Six Years After It Happened: A Daughter's Memoir of Mental Illness* commemorates Lori's terrifying adolescent experience of her mother's psychosis, while *Stories from My Memory-Shelf: Fiction and Essays from My Past* is an autobiographical collection featuring stories and essays inspired by other events from Lori's own life. In the summer of 2014, Lori began work on a second memoir, *The Long Road Home*, during the course of a two-month-long journey across the United States and Canada. She anticipates that it will be ready for publication in 2016.

Lori's first two novels, *My Life with Michael: A Novel of Sex, Beer and Middle Age* and *Just the Three of Us: An Erotic Romantic Comedy for the Commitment-Challenged*, were released early in 2015. She is currently at work on a third novel, a sequel to *Just the Three of Us*. When she isn't writing (which isn't often), Lori enjoys playing ice hockey, attending beer festivals, and spending long afternoons reading at the beach in the sunshine.

For further information on Lori's upcoming projects, please visit her website at http://lorilschafer.com, where you may subscribe to her newsletter or follow her blog. You are also welcome to email her directly at lorilschafer@outlook.com.

"We Are All Miss America"

ON HEARING OF MY MOTHER'S DEATH SIX YEARS AFTER IT HAPPENED: A DAUGHTER'S MEMOIR OF MENTAL ILLNESS

I rose slowly from the table where I'd been studying. Deliberately donned my lavender raincoat, my hands shaking, sweat forming along my hairline like condensation over a steaming pot. Chose my words carefully, not wanting to suggest more than I meant.

"I am going to school."

I nudged past her to the door, placed my hand on the knob, and gave it a yank. She yanked back, all of her considerable might concentrated on the bones of my wrists, dislodging my grip from the door and sending me crashing through the sheetrock, leaving a nearly woman-sized hole in the wall.

"What do you want from me?!" she yelled nonsensically, as if I were a disobedient child having a fit of temper.

"I want my life back!" I shouted, conscious of the melodrama of it, my pathetic cry, but aware, too, that there was no elegant way to express what I wanted. And no hope of making her understand it even if I found the words with which to explain it.

She didn't answer, but swung me forcibly around again, causing me to hit the opposite wall of the foyer sideways, leaving a smaller, skinnier trench in the sheetrock. And then grabbed me by one hand, dragged me out to the car, and threw me inside.

I swallowed, rubbing my wrist, relief flowing through me like a rainshower. I could still make an appearance at school, might still be able to graduate on time and get out of this hellhole once and for all. She backed blindly out of the driveway and took off, far faster than usual. But not in the direction of my school. Towards the border, the state line.

"I could take you away," she'd told me once, smugly, after the first time I'd made a break for it and had to be hauled forcibly home. "Take you to the airport and fly you anywhere I want to; somewhere no one will ever find you. And I am your mother and there is absolutely nothing that anyone could do to stop me." She'd smiled complacently, humming cheerfully under her breath. Pleased with her cleverness, the infallibility of her plan, her power.

I held hard to my seat and harder to my fear. I focused on it, drew strength from it. I didn't speak. In silence I awaited an opportunity, a careless moment, while she screeched around sandy curves, slamming me sideways, partly restrained by the seatbelt that was intended to ensure my safety but which was hemming me in, trapping me in the car with her.

"You want a life?" she snarled unexpectedly as we approached a glaring red stop sign, barely tapping the brakes. "I'll kill us both!"

But my left hand was already on the latch of the belt strapping me into the vehicle; my right hovered by the door handle. I felt her fingers snatching at my jacket as I jumped and rolled uncontrollably out onto the pavement. I heard her cursing violently behind me as the car shuddered to a noisy halt. The backyard backwoods of New England sprawled out before me and I sprinted into them, clawed my way through branches and brambles and pricker-bushes, and came at last to a tall wire fence that I climbed awkwardly, my full-grown feet too large for its twisted footholds, and then jumped, catching my jeans on its pointed peak and tearing them nearly the length of the seam, scraping bits of the soft flesh underneath.

I stopped. Listened. No sound of pursuit came to my ears. I stopped breathing. Listened again. Scanned the sky and tried to judge my direction from the clouds hiding the sun. Took a tentative step, my footfall crackling the underbrush. Listened again and heard nothing. Looked and saw nothing, nothing but trees and bushes and pine needles and the slivered remnants of last autumn's leaves finally freed from the cover of snow.

And then began trudging the miles through the woods back to town...

I was sixteen when my mother became mentally ill. I experienced first-hand the terror of watching someone I loved transform into a monster, the terror of discovering that I was to be her primary victim. For years I've lived with the sadness of knowing that she, too, was a helpless victim – a victim of a terrible disease that consumed and destroyed the strong and caring woman I had once called Mom.

She died in 2007. No one will ever know her side of the story now. But perhaps, at last, it's time for me to tell mine.

On Hearing of My Mother's Death Six Years After It Happened

Now available in paperback (both standard and large print sizes) and eBook from retailers worldwide.

PROLOGUE TO LORI SCHAFER'S FORTHCOMING MEMOIR THE LONG ROAD HOME

"I've taken this road before. So many times have I found myself wandering upon it, this and others like it, countless routes and countless roads, all of them different and all of them the same. Roads to places I have never been and have never wanted to go, roads to towns I know and cities I don't. Roads paved onto every kind of landscape, roads crisscrossing the nation and the globe. Roads that have carried me away and carried me home; roads that have taken me somewhere, taken me everywhere, taken me nowhere.

But this road is the last road. My last road. The last road I will ever take, the last journey I will ever make. It is to be my last road and my longest road. The road I will take until it ends. The long road home."

lorilschafer.com

www.ingramcontent.com/pod-product-compliance
Lightning Source LLC
Chambersburg PA
CBHW020324130626
46549CB00003B/1001